Her Phoenix Heart

CINDY HIDAY

This is a work of fiction. Any similarity to real persons, living or dead, is coincidental and not intended by the author.

Printing History:

Hard Shell Word Factory/April 2003
Booklocker.com, Inc./June 2006

ISBN: 1503072371
ISBN-13: 978-1503072374

Dedicated to
anyone who has dared to dream.

Other Titles by Cindy Hiday

Iditarod Nights

A Bed of Roses

Acknowledgments

This book wouldn't have happened if not for the support and guidance of Dee Lopez and her Professional Writing Workshop. To all my fellow writers who shared their wisdom and laughter, and suffered endless revisions while encouraging me to keep going, a huge thank you. My deepest gratitude to Kimberly A. Cook for allowing me the experience of getting a tattoo without the pain. Service above and beyond! And special thanks to my ever-patient husband and family, who put up with my stubbornness and wild ideas.

Preface

The phoenix is a sacred bird of great beauty, as large as an eagle, yet unique, with feathers of crimson and gold and purple, a long, sweeping tail and jeweled eyes. Stories of the mythical bird have appeared and reappeared through the centuries, the details of its death and rebirth taking on different forms from one account to another. But from its ancient beginnings, the phoenix has always been likened to the sun, ending its day in a crimson fireball and rising golden the following morning.

In the most common of these tales, the rare bird is fabled to live five hundred years in a garden of splendid flowers and crystal springs. As its wings become heavy with age, it builds a nest of spices and herbs high in a date palm, where the heat of the sun sets the twigs afire. With wings outspread, the old phoenix is consumed in the flames. From these ashes, a young phoenix rises with the dawn to welcome a new life. The cycle of death and rebirth is repeated through all eternity. Most revered of mythical birds, the phoenix is a symbol of resurrection and renewal of the human spirit, of rebirth after defeat or desolation.

The phoenix has also been used to describe a person of matchless beauty and goodness.

1

Beth gazed out the window of the limousine at the rain-drenched streets of downtown Portland. There was something about Oregon's 'City of Roses' at night that appealed to her, especially around the holidays. It was two days after Thanksgiving, but Christmas had already made its appearance with the arrival of the seventy-foot Douglas fir at Pioneer Courthouse Square. She was looking forward to seeing the tree decked out in its hundreds of white lights. She could tolerate the man sitting next to her that much longer, she told herself, glancing at him from the corner of her vision.

Ian Heller, a plastic surgeon from Chicago, his eyes glassy and an unhealthy ruddiness to his plump cheeks from several gin and tonics, winked at her. "What do you say we skip the scenic tour and finish our business in my hotel room?"

Beth had to admit his offer didn't surprise her. Though he'd seemed genuinely interested in her work with burn victims at Derma Definitions, and had been cordial over dinner, a voice in the back of her head had told her Dr. Ian Heller was no more interested in seeing Christmas lights than she was in visiting his hotel room. But she'd wanted to give Dr. Rivers's colleague the benefit of the doubt.

So much for professional courtesy.

She was about to tell the good doctor what he could do with his suggestion when his clammy fingers slid under the hem of her wool skirt and clamped onto her thigh. Drawing a startled gasp, Beth slapped his hand away and slid to the forward seat.

"Touch me again," she said coldly, "and I'll break your hand."

"Is everything all right?" the chauffeur asked through the open partition directly behind her.

Beth's heart thudded, once. The man who'd introduced himself moments earlier as Tyler Stone had a voice as deep and lush as the velvet interior of his fancy car. When he'd emerged from the sleek, white limousine, his garrison cap pulled low over his eyes, his black uniform emphasizing long legs and broad shoulders, Beth had stared. *Now there's trouble*, she remembered thinking for no apparent reason.

She slanted Ian a frown. At the moment, Tyler Stone was the least of her worries. Swallowing against the tight anger lodged in her throat, she addressed the driver. "I'd like you to drop me off at the nearest light-rail station, please."

Tyler Stone brought the car to a stop at a red light. He turned and Beth got her first good look at his eyes, a flash of burnished steel in the bright lights of a shop on the corner. They were a sharp contrast to his short, coal black hair and slashed brows. Experienced. Shrewd. *As if he can read my every thought*. Beth felt a flush of heat that lingered, even as he looked away.

"Yes, ma'am," he said, and the car started moving again.

Beth breathed a sigh of relief and settled back in the seat. It was a beautiful car, plush burgundy upholstery, polished oak accents, a sunroof, cellular phone, television, DVD and God only knew what else. *Too bad I'm not going to have time to enjoy it.*

She made herself look at the man sitting across from her. "It's been an interesting evening," she told him, "but this is where I get out."

Ian had the audacity to look hurt. Under different circumstances his protruding lower lip might have been comical.

"The evening's young yet. Where will you go?" he asked.

"Home. Alone." Beth repositioned her black felt tam on her head, snugged the front of her belted wool jacket, and muttered, "While I still have some dignity intact."

"But, honey—"

"I am not your honey!" Bile rose in Beth's throat. *Dr. Rivers is definitely going to hear about this!* Her hand went to her side for her purse, but it wasn't there. She'd left it on the seat next to Ian in her haste to escape his grope. She reached for it and the doctor grabbed her wrist.

"Not so fast," he said, his voice thick.

Fear jagged through Beth, settled like a drum beat in her ears. "Let go of me," she stated, trying desperately to control the sudden quaver in her voice.

Instead, the doctor yanked on her wrist. Beth gave an involuntary yelp and landed on the floor at his feet. She felt the carpet tear her hose, the burn of abraded skin on her knees.

"We have unfinished business." Ian pushed his face close to hers.

His breath reeked of soured alcohol. He'd apparently had a lot more to drink than Beth had realized. His fingers dug into her wrist, but she resisted the impulse to fight his hold, knowing she was no match against his strength. But, oh, how she hated his arrogant attempt to control the situation. To control *her*. Her stomach plunged sickeningly as it all came back to her—the explosive moods, the threats, the humiliation.

And with the memory came cold, calculating rage. *Not this time. Never again.* Then her friend Samantha's advice raced through her head. *Confuse your attacker. It could buy you time to get free.*

Beth decided if it worked for a woman who moonlighted as a nightclub bouncer, sometimes ejecting disorderly patrons twice her size, it was worth a try. She drew in a steadying breath, met Ian's drunken gaze, and smiled. It felt stiff and unnatural, as if her face would crack from the effort, but amazingly the doctor's grip loosened. Beth silently counted to three and jerked her arm back.

But instead of breaking free, as she'd hoped,

the doctor retightened his hold. The momentum of her arm caused him to lurch toward her. Acting on reflex, Beth slammed the heel of her free hand into his face.

Ian let out a curdling howl. The limousine skidded to a halt and the doctor shot from the seat and landed on top of Beth, pinning her to the floor.

She struggled to breathe beneath his considerable girth. "Get off me you son of—"

A gust of cold air brushed her legs and the weight lifted as Ian Heller was pulled from the car.

"What the—" he sputtered, trying to get his feet under him. He landed on his rump on the wet pavement between two parked cars.

Tyler Stone braced his legs and hoisted the doctor to his feet as if he were no more than a bag of hot air. Ian jerked free. His nose was bleeding. From the floor of the limousine, Beth watched the two men face off at the edge of the road in the pouring rain, the street lamp spotlighting them as though they were on stage.

"What the hell do you think you're doing?" Ian raged. "You were paid to chauffeur, not chaperone!"

"Then act like a man instead of an

irresponsible ass."

The chauffeur's voice was as hard as the look in his eyes and a shudder rippled through Beth. As much as Ian Heller may have deserved it, she hoped he wasn't stupid enough to physically attack the tall man in black. Something in the way Mr. Stone carried himself told her he had been in his share of fights. And he was used to winning.

Not that she'd been any easier on the good doctor.

Ian chose that moment to lift a hand to his upper lip. "I'm bleeding!" He looked from the red stain on his fingers to Beth. "You little bitch!"

He took a lunging step toward the car, but Tyler had anticipated the man's move and slammed the door shut.

Heller whirled on him, angry indignation contorting his features. Tyler tasted metal and realized he was grinding the fillings in his teeth. He'd met men like Heller before. Self-important. Egotistical. Crude. He stood his ground, almost wishing the man would take a swing at him. Nobody talked to one of his passengers that way. And nobody manhandled a woman in the back of his limousine. He eyed Heller's bloodied nose and resisted a smirk.

Even if that woman is capable of defending herself.

He had to admit he wouldn't have expected it of the petite woman he'd escorted to the limo. With legs that made a man look twice, he'd thought Elizabeth Heart alluringly delicate in her neat wool suit, her little cap barely containing a fire-storm of red-gold hair, her small chin held high. She'd almost made him forget about the rain slicker he'd left home, or the fact that Dan O'Connor, his relief driver, was supposed to have taken this job tonight.

Apparently Heller had misread the woman as well. Tyler studied the paunchy little man's combative stance and cursed Dan's timing. "You going to do it, or not?" he asked impatiently.

Uncertainty flicked across Heller's expression. "You've got no right tossing me out like that."

"It's my car."

"Dr. Rivers will hear about this. You can expect him to demand a full refund."

"He won't have to," Tyler said, relieved the threat was gone. He'd never enjoyed settling matters with his fists, even when it had been the only way. "I'll have his money in the mail by morning."

A small group of passers-by had gathered on the sidewalk a few feet away to gawk. Tyler pulled a white handkerchief from his hip pocket and thrust it at Heller, causing him to flinch. "Clean yourself up."

The doctor snatched the handkerchief and pressed it to his nose. "How the hell am I supposed to get back to my hotel?"

Tyler reached into his trouser pocket, pulled out a quarter and flipped it in Heller's direction. "Call a cab."

Heller caught the coin, his fingers forming a fist around it, and for an instant Tyler thought he might have to fight the man after all.

Then the doctor jammed the quarter in the pocket of his suit jacket and said, "You're a sorry son of a bitch, you know that?"

Tyler gave a smile that held no humor. "I've been called worse." Mostly by his own father, but that was none of this man's business.

Heller stepped up onto the sidewalk and mumbled a parting four-letter suggestion of what Tyler could do to himself. Tyler chose to ignore it.

With the doctor's departure, the gawkers began to disperse. Some looked disappointed that the argument had ended without a single blow. Tyler tipped his head back and closed his eyes, letting the rain pelt his face. His uniform was soaked, he'd lost a paying client, and his land-yacht of a car was blocking traffic. A perfect evening to match the perfect afternoon he'd had arguing with his daughter. Combing his fingers through his wet hair, he skirted the limo and got in.

The fragrance of roses embraced him immediately. He caught a glimpse of fire and gold in the rearview mirror and realized Ms. Heart had returned to the forward seat. Her face shone pale in the dome light, her green eyes stark. A small diamond stud winked from one ear. Tyler pulled his door shut, throwing the interior of the car in shadow.

"Are you all right?" he asked.

"Oh, I'm just great."

Tyler heard the unsteadiness beneath her sharp tone. "Do you need a doctor?"

His lovely passenger gave an inelegant snort. "I've had my fill of doctors for one evening, thank you."

The remark brought a rueful smile to Tyler's lips. "You and me both, lady." He eased the big car into the flow of traffic. He'd told himself it was none of his business, but couldn't stop from saying, "I hope this guy wasn't a friend of yours."

"No. He was no friend."

Beth leaned back in the seat and hugged herself as the city lights funneled away from her through the smoked rear window. She suddenly couldn't seem to get warm. She made to smooth her hair and discovered her tam was gone. She reached down and searched the shadowed floor. As her fingers touched the soft felt, a truck pulled up behind the limousine, its headlights flooding the back so that Beth could clearly see the rip in her hose and the rug burn on her right knee. A moan of angry frustration rose in her throat. *How could I have been so gullible?*

"What is it?" the chauffeur asked.

The alarm in his voice only intensified Beth's humiliation. *I'm 31, for God's sake! I know better.*

The car stopped and Tyler Stone turned. "What's wrong?" he demanded.

"The creep ruined my nylons." Angry tears pressed at the backs of her eyes.

"I'm sorry."

She hadn't expected him to understand, but when she met his gaze in the lights of the truck still behind them, she saw the sympathy in his burnished eyes gone soft. Kindness. In spite of her earlier premonition about the man, she realized she felt safe with him. A lump swelled in her throat.

"You handled yourself pretty good back there," he said, his voice low and velvet-edged.

Beth swallowed hard and tried to smile, but couldn't quite. "Have you been in many fights, Mr. Stone?"

"Call me Tyler. I've been in enough."

"Then maybe you can tell me how to stop shaking."

Something dark flicked across his expression, but his tone was gentle as he advised, "Take deep breaths. It'll pass."

The truck honked to let them know the light had changed. Tyler faced front and they were moving again. "Where do you live?"

"Just drop me off at the Square."

"I can't do that."

Beth massaged the growing ache in her temple. "Then the nearest bus stop."

"I'm not going to dump you on some street corner and ruin what's left of my evening worrying about you."

The curtness in his response drew her gaze again. In spite of the muscle that clenched in his jaw, he had a fascinating face. There was a deceiving innocence to his firm, sensual mouth and the way his straight nose tipped up almost imperceptibly at the end. Deceiving because she'd seen the passion in his anger. He was a man used to having things his way. And right now, his anger was directed at her. Yet, oddly, she wasn't frightened.

"Why would you worry about me?" she asked quietly, and was surprised at his muttered oath.

"Not all of us are like Heller."

Us, meaning men. Beth understood then and felt it tug at her conscience. He was trying to help her, trying to be chivalrous, and she hadn't even bothered to thank him. A wry smile tugged at her mouth. Chivalry. Tyler Stone and his white 'steed' had come to her rescue. If she hadn't been so tired, she might have laughed at the whole crazy situation.

She gave him her address in the northeast Hollywood district and let the velvety interior of the car pull her into its warmth. *Definitely more comfortable than the city bus.*

"I'm grateful for your help," she said. "And I'll reimburse you if Dr. Rivers demands a refund."

"I don't want your money, ma'am."

"What will your employer say to that?"

"You're looking at him."

She hadn't been, but did now. Heat jagged

through her and she looked away. "I don't want to feel I owe you."

Tyler wondered if it was just him she didn't want to be indebted to, or men in general. "You don't owe me a thing."

Long seconds passed before he heard her soft, "Thank you."

The difficulty she had saying it had him guessing it was more than tonight's scrape with Heller that had taught her not to trust. He found himself wanting to know more about the woman behind the tough front.

But time, it would seem, wasn't on his side as she extended her arm through the privacy window and pointed to a house on the right.

"It's that one with Santa in front."

A single-level brick house, like its neighbor on either side, sat tucked against the base of a low butte. Multi-colored Christmas lights framed a covered porch, and a three-foot tall Santa, his illuminated colors faded, stood sentry at the steps. The limousine dwarfed the red Geo and compact pickup parked side by side in front of the wide, two-story garage. A dog, a big one by the sound of it, barked from somewhere in back.

It was still raining hard. Tyler grabbed the umbrella from the floor and got out to open the rear door of the limo. Considering he was already soaked, he didn't bother with his cap.

Expanding the umbrella, he took Elizabeth Heart's hand to help her from the car. It was small and cool and trembled in his and touched some deep need in him to protect. She stood regarding him with those wide green eyes, her hair disheveled and her stockings torn, and he wanted to pull her into his arms and tell her nobody would ever hurt her again.

"I'll walk you to the door," he said.

She drew her hand back, tucking it quickly in the pocket of her short jacket. "That won't be necessary. I'll be fine. Thank you again for the ride."

It came easier this time, as though she'd decided he didn't pose a threat. Tyler was glad of that much at least. "It was my pleasure, Ms. Heart."

Amusement crinkled the corners of her eyes. "It was a hell of an evening, wasn't it?"

Tyler chuckled and pushed his fingers through his hair again. "Yes, ma'am, it was that."

"Well...good night, Tyler." She turned and walked toward the house.

Her belted jacket flared over her slim, rounded hips. Tyler watched their provocative sway, convinced she was unconscious of the effect. He continued to stand beside the limousine long after she'd produced a key and let herself in. His hair lay flat against his head and rivulets of water coursed down his face. He was wet to the skin. But he wasn't cold. Far from it. He felt like he'd been pushed from an airplane without a chute, smack into the middle of a monsoon, and his blood was pumping hard.

Maybe it was her hair, like fire. Or the sound of her voice when she said his name, like aged wine, mellow and potent. Or the smell of her, like sweet, rain-soaked roses, that made him feel as if he'd suddenly lost control of his senses.

No. It's her smile, he decided. He had the feeling she didn't do it often, at least toward a man she'd just met.

The porch light went off, then the Christmas lights and Santa, and Tyler realized she'd probably been watching him from the window. Probably wondering why he was still standing out there like a fool. A wet fool, at that.

Good question.

He climbed into the limousine. He should have been upset over losing a fare, but he wasn't. Meeting the lovely, enigmatic Elizabeth

Heart had made the evening worth every penny.

As he backed the long car out of her driveway, he found himself regretting the fact that he'd probably never see her again.

~~~

"Dad, is that you?"

"Yeah, baby," Tyler answered, coming into the room.

Holly had her long legs curled under her on the couch and was watching TV in her pajamas, a bowl of popcorn on the cushion beside her.

Hardly a baby anymore, Tyler mused. *Hell, she's almost as tall as me and wears a 34B.* But as long as she let him, he would continue to use the nickname he'd given her the day he'd brought her home from the hospital. *Has it really been almost eighteen years?*

His daughter sat up, her long, coffee-colored hair a tangle of curls, mild surprise in her dark eyes. "You're home early. Did your client cancel?"

"Not exactly." Tyler shrugged loose of his wet jacket, then on a weary sigh admitted, "I threw him out."

Holly's eyes widened. "What happened?"

Tyler dropped onto the other end of the old

tweed couch. While he pulled his soggy shoes and socks off, he filled his daughter in on his evening.

When he got to the part where his lovely lady passenger had given Dr. Heller a bloody nose, Holly's jaw dropped. "Are you serious?"

"As a heart attack." Tyler put his bare feet on the coffee table. His toes were wrinkled and white with cold. He laid his head back and closed his eyes.

"You forgot your slicker again, didn't you?"

Tyler's answering grunt was humorless.

"Have some popcorn." He heard Holly scoot the bowl closer. "It'll make you feel better."

Tyler rolled his head and peered at her through a slitted eye. "Is this your dinner?"

"Nooo."

Tyler's gaze sharpened. He was too tired for any more sarcasm tonight.

"I had some of that leftover spaghetti," Holly relented on an exaggerated sigh.

"Good." Tyler felt guilty that he couldn't always have dinner with his daughter. It was one of the disadvantages of being self-employed. Getting ahead meant long hours, even with Dan working for him part-time.

He helped her finish the popcorn and watched the last of the news. More rain was forecast for tomorrow. The college brochures were on the coffee table where he'd left them, untouched. Apparently nothing he'd said to her that afternoon had gotten through. After the sports report, he clicked off the television.

"So, have you given any more thought to what we discussed earlier?" he asked.

Holly cast him a self-suffering look. "*I* discussed, *you* yelled."

"Holly—"

But she didn't wait for him to finish. "How can I decide which college to go to when I don't know what I want to major in?"

Tyler had heard the argument before. "There are a lot of opportunities in the medical field," he suggested, for what must have been the hundredth time. He couldn't help it. He liked the sound of Holly Louise Stone, M.D. Although after meeting Dr. Heller tonight, maybe he'd push for dentistry instead. It occurred to him that he didn't know what Elizabeth Heart did for a living. She'd said Dr. Heller wasn't a friend. Did that mean they were connected professionally?

"Maybe I'll be a rocket scientist," Holly grumbled.

"You'd make a good one."

"Dad—"

"I know," he interrupted, his smile bland, "you were just kidding." He caught and held her gaze. "But I'm not. You're smart enough to be anything you want."

"But I don't *know* what I want! Why do I have to decide now? Why can't I just get a job, like you did?"

Tyler clamped down hard on his impatience. "We've been over this before, Holly. Grandma Lou left you that money so you could go to college and do better."

The fact that he had dropped out of school his senior year wasn't something he was proud of, even if his motives had been honorable. He had a pretty good idea where he'd have ended up if he hadn't made the decision to claim responsibility for his baby daughter, if he'd allowed Holly's mother to put their child up for adoption. Probably a jail cell somewhere, instead of the house his mother had been raised in. He'd been a seventeen-year-old delinquent with an attitude problem and parents who didn't care.

"But you've got your own business now," Holly argued. "You did fine without going to college."

"I got lucky. And I worked a lot of crummy jobs for minimum wage. I don't want that for you."

"You can't protect me forever, Dad."

"Maybe not," Tyler replied, the edge to his voice softening, "but I can see that you get the education you need to take care of yourself."

Once again, he found himself thinking of Elizabeth, wondering if her knowledge of self-defense had been instinct or learned. He tempered the unbidden anger that shot through him. A woman shouldn't have to use force to tell a man she wasn't interested.

He looked at Holly. What would *she* have done in a situation like that? The fact that he didn't know settled uneasy in his stomach. Maybe he should teach his daughter some of the things he'd learned on the street. But some of the things he'd learned, he hoped she never found out about.

"Actually, I was thinking of waitressing at the Meatmarket Restaurant," Holly commented in an off-handed tone.

"Over my dead body!"

His daughter shot him a mischievous smile. "Honestly, Dad, you have no sense of humor."

2

Beth was still fuming the following afternoon as she suffered Samantha's attempt to instruct her in baking Christmas cookies.

"I was humiliated!" she said, giving the cookie cutter a savage twist. She hated that the most. How many times had she been degraded and embarrassed in public by the man she'd vowed to 'love, honor and cherish'?

Bo Diddley, her three-year-old German shepherd, sat at her feet and gave a nervous whimper. Beth met the anxiety in his big, doleful eyes. "It's okay, sweetie, mom's not mad at you."

"I can't believe Dr. John would set you up like that." Samantha turned from the oven, her tawny eyes flashing. The thin scar that ran from brow to cheek, indistinguishable under normal conditions, stood out pale against her heightened color. "If you ask me, he deserves a good punch in the nose, too."

Beth had no doubt Sam would do it, given the opportunity. At five-foot eight, her twenty-six-year old friend was lean and solid in black spandex shorts and matching tank top. How she could put in eight to ten hours, five days a week, at Derma Definitions, moonlight at Juliet's Night Club, sometimes six evenings out of seven, and still find time to workout was beyond Beth. No, it definitely wouldn't be good for business to turn Samantha Dixon loose on their unsuspecting colleague, even if he did deserve it.

That's what didn't make sense. From the first day she'd approached Dr. John Rivers with the concept of using tattooing to compliment his cosmetic surgery practice, he'd been enthusiastic, professional, and courteous. His patient referrals over the past three years had been instrumental in making Derma Definitions a success. Beth didn't want to believe he would have knowingly "set her up," as Sam put it. There had to be a logical explanation. Come tomorrow, she'd insist on it.

"Let me handle Dr. Rivers," she said.

Sammy grinned. "The way you handled Dr. Heller?"

Beth returned the grin and winked. "Only if diplomacy doesn't work."

She placed the last cookie on the sheet and wiped her hands down the thighs of her faded blue jeans. The front of her indigo turtleneck was dusted with flour and white fingerprints dotted the sleeves where she'd pushed them up. Bo let out an impatient woof and slapped the black and white tiled floor with his tail. Beth looked down at him and he wiggled his haunches like a fidgety child.

But it was Sammy who knelt and wrapped her arms around the dog's broad neck. "Are you ready for some of Auntie Sam's fabulous Christmas cookies?"

Bo's long tail whipped the floor. His gaze darted from Sammy to Beth to the white Formica counter, his tongue sliding over his chops as if already savoring the freshly baked confections. It made Beth feel a bit guilty. She was a mediocre cook, at best. Anything from scratch was something novel for both of them. She believed in can-openers and microwaves, but Sammy seemed determined to prove survival was possible without those timesaving tools.

Her friend straightened and checked the oven. "It's ready," she said and reached for the cookie sheet. But one look at the twisted Santas and she burst into laughter.

"Oh for Heaven's sake." Beth snatched the sheet off the counter and took it to the oven. "If I'd known you were going to be such a critic, I never would have agreed to waste my Sunday this way." She slid the sheet into the oven and closed the door. Setting the timer, she turned and leaned against the counter, folding her arms across her middle. "What really burns me about last night is that I lost one of my diamond earrings."

Sammy immediately sobered. "Not the ones your parents gave you?"

Beth nodded. The diamond studs had been a gift from her mom and dad when she'd entered college, a symbol of the bright future ahead of her. They'd been among the few personal possessions she'd taken with her when she'd fled her husband.

"Have you reported it to the police?" Sammy asked.

"No. I'm almost positive I lost it when the good doctor and I were rolling around in the back of the limousine."

"Call the service. Maybe the driver found it."

Beth had thought of that, but hadn't summoned the courage to follow through. She was apprehensive about seeing Tyler Stone again. There was something intensely compelling about him that frightened and excited her. From behind the lace curtains of her darkened living room, she'd watched him stand in the rain and stare at the house. Part of her wanted to know more about the tall man in black, while another part, that part of her she kept carefully tucked away, was convinced she'd been looking at a man who could leave her vulnerable to everything she'd steered clear of since her divorce.

She shook the disturbing thought from her head. "You're right. I'll call this afternoon."

The timer went off and she turned to remove the cookies from the oven. She'd rolled the dough unevenly and the thinner cookies had burned edges. She glared at Sammy as she carried them to the counter.

"One word and you'll wear them."

Sammy clamped her mouth shut and held her hands up in feigned surrender.

Beth tossed a cookie to Bo Diddley. He caught it in midair, his jaw champing noisily. "Somebody appreciates my effort," she said, her tone smug.

Sammy made a face. "Bo would eat dirt if you put enough sugar on it. You'd better let me finish those."

"You won't get any argument from me." Beth moved to the bar that separated the kitchen from the dining area and planted her bottom on one of the tall, oak stools.

Sam rolled out more sugar dough and casually asked, "So, was the limo driver cute?"

Beth felt her face warm. "I didn't notice."

"Liar. Come on, Bethie. The man saved you from evil Dr. Heller's clutches. How could you not notice what he looked like?"

He'd looked angry.

And he'd said he would worry about her if she didn't allow him see her home. The last man to worry about her like that had been her father.

"First of all, I didn't need saving."

"And?"

"He was tall, dark and devastatingly handsome," Beth answered impatiently. She propped her elbows on the counter and rested her chin in her hands. "Satisfied?"

Sammy shoved the cookie sheet into the oven and leaned across the bar, grinning. "No. Tell me more."

Beth groaned. "You never give up, do you?"

"Face it, Bethie, your love life is nonexistent."

"I date."

"Yeah, right."

Beth considered arguing the matter, but knew she'd only lose. She'd had her share of encounters after her divorce—had insisted on it, in fact, driven by a need to reclaim her sexuality. But they'd been men of her choosing. Physically attractive, considerate, single men. Men immune to emotional commitment.

Disposable.

But over time, the dates had become fewer and fewer. Her work with derma pigmentation and her patients had become the dominating factor in her life. Except for last night's fiasco, Beth couldn't remember the last time she'd gone out with a man.

She gave Sam a restless frown. "Didn't you say you had to work at Juliet's this afternoon?"

"Yes—and you're changing the subject." Sam glanced at the clock above the stove and pushed away from the counter. "Lucky for you, if I don't go now, I'll be late."

Beth walked her friend to the door and gave her a hug. "Thanks for the cookies."

"Any time." Sam darted out the door, into a

torrent of rain. Sprinting across the soggy lawn toward her studio apartment above the garage, she hollered, "Save some for me!"

"No way!" Beth shouted back, and closed the door on Sammy's answering laughter.

She was in the kitchen, sharing another cookie with Bo, when the doorbell rang. Beth frowned, then spotted Sammy's black sweatshirt lying on the counter. She smiled and shook her head. Sammy had a key to the house, but evidently she'd forgotten that, too.

Grabbing the sweatshirt, she dashed back into the front room with Bo at her heels. Laughing, she opened the door to a gust of cool, damp air and tossed the shirt at the person standing under cover of the porch.

It wasn't Sammy.

Tyler Stone caught the sweatshirt as it bounced off his chest. "Thanks," he said, holding it up assessingly, "but I don't think it'll fit."

He wore a bulky sweater with a geometric pattern of bright southwestern colors. Golds, russets and turquoise. Black jeans hugged his long, lean legs and came down over the tops of a pair of western-cut leather boots.

But it was the contrast between his coal black hair and pale gray eyes that captured

Beth's attention. In the overcast afternoon, the effect was even more striking than it had been the evening before. She didn't want to stare, but his eyes were like magnets drawing her in. Her earlier premonition of vulnerability had not been a figment of her imagination, she decided. There was something about this man that made her feel naked when he looked at her, not just physically, but emotionally. Her heart gave an uncomfortable thud.

Bo Diddley growled deep in his throat.

"It's okay," Beth murmured.

The big dog quieted, but his ears remained alert, his stance rigid. *He doesn't believe me any more than I do.*

"Will he bite?" Tyler asked, his voice calm.

As if he weren't the least bit threatened. Yet he had the sense not to approach Bo uninvited. Beth gave him credit for that. She gave her pulse another second to return to normal before answering.

"Only if I tell him to."

Tyler Stone smiled. *Oh, Lord, the man has dimples. Deep, gorgeous dimples.* Beth felt her pulse take another jolt. *Stop staring, for God's sake!* She forced her eyes to shift away and realized he still held Sam's sweatshirt.

"I apologize for throwing that at you," she

said, taking the shirt from him. "I thought you were someone else."

"The shirt's owner, no doubt."

"My renter, Samantha. She was helping me bake cookies and left it on the counter." Beth pressed her lips together before she babbled any more information that was really none of his business.

"That explains it."

Beth gave a small frown. "Excuse me?"

"The flour on your clothes."

"Oh." She made to brush herself off and realized she'd been twisting Sam's sweatshirt into a knot. Tossing it aside, she took a couple of swipes at the front of her turtleneck and succeeded only in spreading the mess. She could feel Tyler Stone watching and it annoyed her. Bracing her hands on her hips, she drew her shoulders back, and asked, "Is there something I can do for you?"

His dark brows lifted innocently. "You didn't call for a limousine?"

Beth tried not to smile, but darn it, it was hard when his gray eyes sparkled at her that way. She looked around him at the black Jeep parked in front of the house. "What limousine?"

He tossed a quick glance over his shoulder,

then looked at her and grinned. "I hate when it does that."

Beth's lips trembled. "I suppose it could be pretty embarrassing at times."

"You have no idea."

She had a full, rich laugh that Tyler found as intoxicating as her voice. As the woman herself. Without the heels she'd worn the night before, she barely came to his chin. A neat, sexy package of curves. Her hair was disheveled, like a soft wreath of flame encircling her head. Her green eyes studied him. Like a lioness would study a potential threat. Guarded. Intelligent. And not to be messed with. They stirred a primal heat deep inside him.

And she was waiting for him to tell her what he was doing here. He reached into his jeans pocket and held the tiny, sparkling object out to her.

"I believe this belongs to you?"

The immediate pleasure in her expression made Tyler glad he'd decided to come. It wasn't that he hadn't wanted to return the earring, but he hadn't been sure he was ready for the way this woman single-handedly dominated his thoughts. He wasn't used to that.

Her fingers brushed the palm of his hand as she took the diamond stud from him and a small electrical charge shot up his arm. If she'd felt it too, she was careful to hide it. She made a fist around the earring and clutched it to her breast.

"Thank you," she said quietly. "You have no idea how much these mean to me."

When she lifted her gaze to his, Tyler's heart constricted. He knew. He wondered if she was aware of how sad and lost and exposed she looked at that moment.

"You're welcome," he replied in a voice gone rough.

She looked away to carefully tuck the diamond in the front pocket of her jeans. When her gaze returned to his, her features were once more smooth, her emotions tucked away as neatly as her earring. She stepped back and pulled the door wide.

"Come in before you catch a chill."

Her invitation surprised him. The woman wore her privacy like a shield. Tyler entered a cozy room of deep, over-stuffed furnishings, pastels and muted pink roses. Their fragrance, *her* fragrance, vied with the warm, sweet smell of cookies baking. For some reason, he'd expected something a little less tame.

He felt the German shepherd's cold, wet nose touch the back of his hand and stood still, allowing the dog to investigate, without trying to pet him. He had a deep respect for dogs and the protective bond they had with their owners. And he'd noticed this was the first time the shepherd had left Beth's side. He knew without being told that if he threatened this woman, or made any sudden moves, he could easily lose a finger, if not his whole hand.

"Bo, sit."

The command was delivered in a low, even tone, but the dog immediately obeyed. He positioned himself between the stranger and his owner, apparently sensing the latter's unease. Beth had invited him in, but that didn't mean she was comfortable with it, Tyler decided.

"Can I get you a cup of coffee?" she asked.

He was tempted. He wanted to stay. He wanted to discover everything there was to know about this complex lady, explore her layer by layer.

He wanted to kiss her, he realized. Kiss her long and hard, until the tiny frown that had appeared on her otherwise flawless forehead was gone.

"Thank you, but I can't stay. I have a client later this afternoon."

The relief in her expression was so subtle that if he hadn't been paying attention, he would have missed it.

"I appreciate you taking time from your busy schedule to return my earring," she said. "I seem to be indebted to you once again."

"You don't owe me anything, Elizabeth. Returning things my clients leave in the back of the limo is part of my job."

"I didn't mean—"

"Why is it so hard to accept that I might want to do something for you just for the hell of it?"

Because that would make you too dangerous, Beth thought. She'd been a fool to invite him in, to think she could relax with him standing so close. The awareness in his burnished eyes when he looked at her tugged at an unexplained longing. It would be too easy to be seduced by those eyes, to get lost in them. She couldn't allow that to happen.

"Everyone has a hidden agenda," she said.

She could see her comment wasn't what he'd expected. He looked at her as though he would look into her very soul, if he were able to. And for just an instant, she got the feeling he could. She felt the wall she'd carefully constructed around her emotions being torn down, brick by brick. Carefully guarded secrets being slowly exposed. And she was helpless to do anything about it.

Then he was looking over her shoulder, his dark brows pulled low on his forehead. "Something's burning."

Me, Beth thought inanely. Her blood felt like a river of fire through her veins. Then she smelled it, too.

"Ohmygosh!"

She whirled and ran to the kitchen, nearly tripping over Bo Diddley. Without thinking, she yanked open the oven door and grabbed for the cookie sheet. Her unprotected fingers touched hot metal. Crying out, she jerked back and collided with Tyler. Before her mind had a chance to register the unexpected contact with his tall, hard frame, he'd seized her hand and was propelling her toward the sink. He turned on the cold water and plunged her fingers under its stream.

"Sam must have forgotten to set the timer," Beth muttered, trying to focus on the soothing effect of the water on her stinging digits. But the disturbing intimacy of Tyler's body so close to hers made it difficult. The brush of his solid thigh, her shoulder against his arm, the clean smell of his thick black hair, his hand cradling hers. She felt like one of her cookies—soft and warm inside. She might have laughed at the thought if she'd had breath left in her to make sound.

He turned off the water and gave her the dishtowel that hung from a nearby hook. "Dry your hand," he instructed.

"Thank you, but I can..."

He didn't seem to be listening. He turned off the oven, then reached for the aloe plant, the one Sammy had insisted every kitchen needed, on the sill over the sink and twisted off a stem. Before Beth could react, he'd taken her hand again and was squeezing the cool, thick pulp over her red fingers.

"How's that feel?"

"Wonderful." Beth gulped. Wonderfully sensual. His hands were gentle for their size. She pulled from his grasp, afraid he'd notice the rapid trip of her pulse in her wrist.

"Thank you, but I'll be fine now."

There it was again, Tyler thought, the shadow of an unhealed wound in her expression. He rocked back on his heels and studied her. "Have you always been this independent?"

He saw her stiffen. "I've learned not to rely on others."

The defiant lift of her narrow chin and the look in her eyes warned Tyler not to pursue the subject. But he did anyway. "Spoken like someone who's had more than just her hand burned," he observed softly.

The fine contours of her jaw sharpened. "I've had my share of life's lessons."

Tyler could have said something to this, but didn't. He had the feeling she was on the verge of telling him to leave, and he wasn't ready to do that yet. "See a doctor if that blisters," he said instead.

Relief, subtle, but there nevertheless, eased the edge of tension in her pale, smooth features. "You're good at emergency first aid."

"It comes with being a father."

It hadn't occurred to Beth he might be married. Why was that? she wondered. And he has a child. Or children. She was fond of children, as long as they were someone else's. She'd never had a desire for any of her own. Bo Diddley satisfied any maternal instincts that might have tried to sway her decision, as had the two cats before him.

"That must put your wife's mind at ease," she said.

"I'm not married."

Divorced. That's just as bad. Divorces left bitter memories. Scars.

"Never have been," he informed her. Then at the confusion that must have registered in her expression, his easy smile deepened. "It's a long story."

Beth didn't know which was more arresting, his dimples or his eyes. Thankfully he turned away, giving her a moment to regain her equilibrium. She watched as he grabbed a potholder, slid the cookie sheet out of the oven and carried it to the garbage. Bo rushed to investigate.

Tyler smiled at the shepherd. "Sorry, fella. I don't think even your digestion could handle these."

Bo cocked his head to one side, his big brown eyes wide, as if to better comprehend the stranger and his words. Beth was amazed to see his tail wagging.

"You're good with dogs," she said. "Is that from experience, as well?"

"Unfortunately, no." Tyler deposited the empty cookie sheet in the sink and tossed the potholder onto the counter. "I've never had time to give a pet the attention it would need."

"I suppose not, what with a family and a

business." Beth cringed. His personal life was none of her concern.

But regardless of what he might say, she did owe him. She knew better than to offer him money, so she pulled a small paper bag from a drawer and put a dozen cookies in it, careful to choose the ones Sam had baked.

"What's this for?" Tyler asked, taking the bag when she thrust it toward him.

She shrugged. "Everything. Giving me a ride last night, returning my earring, the first aid. It isn't much—"

"It's perfect. Thank you."

Beth smiled. How could she not, when he turned those gorgeous dimples on her? *He really does have an attractive face.*

"I'd like to get to know you better," he said.

Beth's smile faded, old fears and uncertainties slipping back into place. She looked away. "I'm not sure that's such a good idea."

"It isn't Heller, is it? Because if it is—"

She laughed in spite of herself. "No, it isn't Heller."

"Are you married?"

"No."

But she has been, Tyler realized. Or something close to it. It was written in her expression like a bad story. And she wasn't ready to pick up the book again.

He stepped closer and saw her resist the urge to back away. *She hates that. She hates being weak.* Tyler respected her tangle of emotions and stopped.

"Is it me you're afraid of?" he asked, his voice low.

"No."

She was lying. Her long amber lashes dipped, her eyes not quite meeting his. Tyler lifted his hand to her cheek. He heard her small intake of breath, but she didn't pull away from his touch. He was glad. Her skin was like satin beneath his fingertips.

"Who did this to you?" he murmured.

"I don't know what you mean."

"You make a lousy liar, Elizabeth."

Startled, she looked at him, her lips parting slightly. God, how he wanted to shape his mouth to them. He knew they would taste as sweet as they looked. Just as he knew she'd bolt if he moved too fast. His fascination with this elusive woman stunned him. Who was she? And what was this strange hold she seemed to have on him?

"Call me Beth," she said, her voice unsteady. "And I think you'd better go now."

Still, she didn't pull away. Tyler realized she was leaving it up to him to make the next move. That alone gave him the strength to release her. He needed her trust.

"I think you're right," he said.

He let her walk him to the front room, her dog following close behind. Tyler welcomed the damp air that cooled his skin when she opened the door. Then he turned and looked at her and the heat returned.

"This isn't over," he told her. "You know that, don't you?"

A multitude of emotions crossed her heart-shaped face. Fear, uncertainty, desire. And finally, determination.

"It has to be," she whispered, and softly closed the door.

3

Beth switched off the Spaulding, a pen-like instrument with a small air-driven motor on top, and gave her patient a reassuring smile. "Just a little longer, Dianne. How are you feeling?"

The forty-eight year old divorced mother of two looked up from her reclined position in the dentist-style chair, a determined set to her mouth. "Like I've got a bad sunburn."

"That's normal," Beth assured her. "It's the needles injecting the color under your skin." She patted the woman's hands wrapped tightly around a smooth stone. "Remember, channel the pain into the stone. When we're done, I'll give you some ointment for the treated area."

The soft blue sheet covering Dianne's upper

body had been pulled down to expose her surgically reconstructed breast following a mastectomy. Using vegetable protein dyes, Beth created a natural-looking aureole. She dipped the needles of the electric tool in a cup of carefully blended pigment and turned the instrument on. Its static-y sound drowned out the melodic variations of a baroque guitar coming from the CD player a short distance away.

She'd designed the studio to put her patients at ease. Shades of dusty blue and rose, framed art on pastel walls, leafy potted plants in the window, and soft music. But there was also a concentrated emphasis on sanitation and safety, autoclave sterilization of implements, individual cups of pigment, and needles that were discarded after each use. The look was clean, airy and professional, right down to Beth's white lab coat and disposable latex gloves.

While she worked, her thoughts returned to yesterday and Tyler's parting words. She'd been unable to get the man out of her head, much to her irritation. There was no point in denying his attractive appeal. All he had to do was look at her with those steel-gray, bedroom eyes and flash her that dimpled smile and she practically melted on the spot.

That was the problem. She refused to become involved with a man who had that kind of power over her. She could lose her identity with a man like Tyler Stone. There would be nothing casual, or disposable, about his kind of relationship.

So there would be no relationship, she told herself.

She turned off the Spaulding and set it aside. Giving the excess dye a final dab with cotton gauze, she brought the back of her patient's chair up. "We're all done."

"That didn't take long."

Beth smiled and removed her gloves. "But I bet you're relieved it's over." She drew a hand-held mirror from the drawer next to her. "It'll look like a stop sign for a few days," she warned, "but the color will fade by a third as the outer layer of your skin sloughs off."

Dianne nodded and studied her image. "I know you showed me photographs of others..." She looked at Beth. Gratitude brimmed her eyes. "I feel normal again. Thank you."

The phoenix spread its wings and rose from its ashes, reborn.

"You're very welcome," Beth replied.

As often happened at moments like this, her

thoughts went to her father. As a plastic surgeon, he'd realized the need for introducing pigments in his field. They'd had long discussions on the subject, planning.

If only he'd lived to see his vision become reality.

If only she hadn't gotten married.

Beth suppressed the acute sense of loss and regret time had yet to heal and drew her thoughts back to the present. "Speaking of photographs," she produced a digital camera from the drawer behind her, "I'd like a couple of 'after' photos to go with the ones I took before we started."

A short time later, Beth had applied a protective gauze bandage to the newly pigmented area and Dianne put her loose-fitting blouse back on.

"In three hours, take the bandage off and apply a thin coating of this." Beth handed her a tube of ointment and a page of instructions.

"How long will it take to heal?"

"Three to six days. It's all there in the instructions. But if you have any problems, don't hesitate to give me a call. See my associate, Marie, on your way out. She'll schedule a follow up appointment for you."

"I'll do that. Thank you again."

Seconds later, Sammy swept into the room, her lab coat flapping behind her. She dropped into the empty chair and groaned. "Lordy, what a day. And it's only Monday."

"How'd it go with Mr. Emerson?"

"Carl Emerson has eyebrows to be proud of," Sammy replied. "His only problem now is explaining how they grew back."

Sam's patient had alopecia, the permanent loss of body hair. He'd adjusted to being bald, but felt he looked odd without eyebrows. Using small needles, fine lines could be drawn in to give the illusion of brow hairs. It was a procedure Beth had taught Sam early in her apprenticeship.

"I spoke with Dr. Rivers today," Beth said, turning to put the camera away.

"Oh? What'd he have to say for himself?"

"He seemed genuinely shocked at Dr. Heller's actions and assured me he'd had no idea the man would try such a thing when he set up our meeting." Beth pushed the drawer closed and leaned a hip against the edge of the cabinet. "It seems Ian Heller divorced about a year ago. Apparently, he's having some sort of male identity crisis."

Sammy rolled her eyes. "Wonderful."

"Anyway, Dr. Rivers apologized and asked

if there was anything he could do to make it up to me."

"An all expenses paid trip to Hawaii would be nice."

Beth smiled. "Sorry, kiddo. I told him his continued referrals were all I wanted, and that Dr. Heller was as good as forgotten."

"And what about the chauffeur? Will he get his money?"

"He assured me Tyler Stone has been paid for his services."

Sammy grinned. "How is Tyler?"

"I wouldn't know." The question annoyed Beth. Her friend hadn't missed a single opportunity to remind her that she'd seen his arrival at the house yesterday.

"He hasn't called?" Sam asked, sounding disappointed.

"Why should he?"

"Because he's an attractive single man and you're an attractive single woman."

"I told you, he was returning my earring. The end." Except that she had a suspicion it wasn't going to be that easy.

"He stayed an awfully long time."

Beth shrugged out of her lab coat and hung it in the small closet behind the door. "And if I'm not mistaken, I explained why."

"You tried to set the oven on fire," Sam scolded. "I knew I shouldn't have left you alone in the kitchen."

"I warned you."

"Yeah, well," Sam swung her feet to the floor and sat up, "are you going to see him again?"

"No." But she wanted to, she realized.

Sam pushed out of the chair with an exaggerated sigh. "That's a shame." She crossed the room to the outer office. "He had a nice looking butt."

Beth's mouth fell open. She was amazed to feel the tips of her ears burn.

Sam laughed and wiggled her fingers over her shoulder at her. "Have a nice evening."

~~~

A stout east wind whipped through the courtyard when Beth left the medical complex a short time later. A flattened paper cup and crumpled brown bag skittered through the growing dusk at her. The ever-present odor of auto exhaust had an underlying dank concrete and earth smell to it. Beth brushed her errant hair out of her eyes and raised the collar of her calf-length coat higher. She stole a glance at the black clouds brushing the tops of the surrounding high-rises. With a little luck, she could be on the bus before it started raining again.

Head bowed against the wind, she sprinted across the courtyard, her low-heeled brown pumps rapping smartly in the crisp evening air, and started down the short flight of steps to Park Avenue. Near the bottom, she glanced up and stopped so fast, had it not been for her grip on the wrought iron railing, her momentum would have carried her tumbling down the remaining step.

A long white limousine was parked at the curb directly in front of her.

The odds that it belonged to Tyler Stone were practically nonexistent, she told herself. There were pages of limousine services in the phone book. The long cars were a common sight in downtown Portland. And yet Beth found herself glancing around for a place to hide.

Traffic cleared and the driver's door opened. Even with his garrison cap pulled low, Beth knew it was him. She stopped breathing. Darn it, no man had a right to look that good in a uniform, she thought with dismay. He came around the limousine, his easy stride that of a man comfortable with his height.

He looked up and saw her. A broad smile dimpled his handsome face. Beth's knees weakened. *Trapped, like a mouse that stayed too long contemplating the cheese.* She tightened her grip on the cold iron railing and willed her mouth to respond.

He touched the brim of his cap and gave her a small nod before turning to open the door for his passenger. *Sammy's right. He does have a nice butt.*

Beth knew if she left now it would make her look like a snob, or a coward, neither of which appealed to her. So she found a place out of the way of the steps, thrust her hands into the deep pockets of her trenchcoat, and waited.

A woman who appeared to be in her late fifties, wrapped in a full-length silver fur, took Tyler's hand and got out of the back of the limousine. Her stark black hair was styled in a short bouffant that defied the wind. A preponderance of rouge high on her cheeks made her face appear ghostly, her crimson lips a harsh slash. But when she looked up at her chauffeur, her features softened, her immediate smile flirtatious. Beth watched in stunned interest as the woman slid a manicured hand along Tyler's lapel, while the other tucked a bill in his jacket pocket. Then she stood on the toes of her dangerously high heels and touched her lips to his cheek.

Patience and kindness edged Tyler's smile as he accepted his client's gratuity. Beth wondered how many other women called on Luxury Coach's services simply for the pleasure of the six-foot tall, dark-haired Tyler Stone's company. The thought brought an unexpected bitter taste to her mouth and she looked away.

"How's your hand?"

His velvet-edged voice, like a warm breeze against her neck, made her jump. Turning, she met the full impact of his eyes. Steel to smoke. They seemed to change with his mood. Or was it her own seesawing emotions clouding her perception?

A heartbeat passed before she could find breath enough to answer him. "It's fine. Thank you."

When Tyler had told her it wasn't over between them, he'd been speaking more from desire than any certainty they'd ever see each other again. But she'd been in his mind. Like an elusive fantasy, she'd drifted through his head, teasing him with her cat-like eyes and fiery hair. It flew about her upturned face now in the brisk evening breeze as if possessing a will of its own. He wondered what it would be like to bury his hands in it, attempt to tame it—to tame her. The aloofness that surrounded her discouraged even the smallest advance, and yet he had the feeling that submerged beneath her cool exterior was a passion made more intriguing by its very inaccessibility.

"Do you believe in fate, Beth?"

His question surprised her, her arched brows lifting. "I don't believe in passively letting fate determine my life," she told him after giving it a moment's thought. "But there are some things—" her voice softened, the tip of her tongue moistening her lips, "—that would seem beyond my control."

"Does that trouble you?"

The flare of awareness in her green eyes an instant before she looked away set off an exquisite ache low in Tyler's gut.

"I prefer to be in control," she said, so quietly he nearly missed it. Then as if impatient with him, or herself, Tyler couldn't be sure which, she took a step back and nodded in the direction his client, Mrs. Peterson, had gone. "Why didn't you let that woman off closer to her destination?"

"She wanted people to admire her new coat."

"She's obviously very fond of you."

"She's a lonely divorcee."

"Who's at least twenty years older than you."

Dear God, what possessed me to say that?

The answer came to her almost immediately. *You could be that lonely woman in another twenty years.*

Tyler's gray eyes narrowed. "Mrs. Peterson pays me to drive her places. Because I show her a little courtesy, she tips well. If you're implying what I think you are—"

"I'm not. I'm sorry."

"You're jealous."

"Don't be ridiculous," she said and quickly glanced away. Then because she felt him watching her, she made herself face him. A reluctant smile tugged at the corners of her mouth. "You might suggest she use a lighter shade of lipstick, though."

At his look of total confusion, Beth laughed. "You have some—" she pointed to her own cheek, "—right about there."

"Oh." He pulled a handkerchief from the back pocket of his trousers and wiped at his face.

Beth shook her head. "You're not rubbing in the right place. Here," she stepped closer and reached for the handkerchief, "let me do it."

It wasn't a smart move. It brought her far

too close to whatever it was about him that was so compelling. Her fingers brushed his when she took the handkerchief from him. A bolt of heat shot up her arm. The cloying fragrance of a woman's jasmine perfume lingered on his jacket. Beth pressed her lips together. She was jealous, darn it. Just a little. She focused her attention on the crimson stain on his cheek and began rubbing.

"Ow! Leave some skin!"

"Don't be such a baby. I've almost got it."

He took her wrist and she froze.

Tyler felt her pulse skip, then race. Knowing he had that affect on her, that she was vulnerable to his touch, was incredibly arousing. He felt his own pulse race to catch up.

"You're trembling," he whispered.

Fear, then irritation flashed in her eyes. Her narrow chin jutted. "It's cold." She pulled her hand from his grasp and gave him back his handkerchief. "If you'll excuse me, I have a bus to catch."

"Let me give you a lift," Tyler said as she turned to go.

"Thanks, but the bus is cheaper."

Tyler suppressed an oath. "I wasn't expecting you to pay, for God's sake." She continued to walk away and he shouted, "Are you always this bull-headed?"

She stopped, her back rigid, and Tyler figured he'd just blown any chance he might have had. *Way to go, Stone.*

Incredibly, amusement flickered in her expression when she turned and looked at him.

"Only toward pushy chauffeurs," she called in return.

Tyler released a long breath. She was like an erratic faucet, running hot and cold at the same time. A gust of wind whipped her long coat against the backs of her legs and lifted her hair in another firestorm of curls around her head. It struck Tyler that he couldn't remember ever feeling as alive as he did at this moment.

It started to rain.

He opened the right front door of the limousine. "Your Luxury Coach awaits."

"What about your client?"

"She's riding home with a friend."

Still, Beth stood her ground. *Damn, the woman can be stubborn.* The wind blew a mist of raindrops up under the brim of Tyler's cap.

"It's not going to change into a Jeep, or maybe a pumpkin on wheels, is it?" she asked.

Tyler grinned. "I can almost guarantee it. Now will you please get in? I don't feel like getting soaked again."

Her laugh was spontaneous and rich. She sprinted toward the car. But before she ducked her head to climb in, she looked up at him and winked. "Go easy on the brakes this time."

Tyler made no answer as he closed the door. How could he when his mouth had gone dry and fire suffused his body? Maybe a cold drenching wouldn't be such a bad idea after all, he thought, making his way to the other side of the car.

The instant he climbed inside, the sky opened and the rain became a torrent. Portland, Oregon—famous for its rivers, roses, and rain. He switched on the headlights and wipers and guided the limo into the flow of rush-hour traffic.

"Tell me," Beth said, pushing her wind-tossed hair from her face, "how do you make any money giving free rides?"

Tyler shot her a wicked smile. "I get good tips."

Her answering laugh was dry. "I'm afraid you're out of luck this time. All I have on me is a bus pass."

"You could always pay me in cookies."

"Hah! You saw what kind of cook I am."

"Then I'll have to come up with something

else."

The implication of his comment hummed in the sudden silence. Beth began fiddling with the heater controls.

"How do you turn this thing down?" she asked, an unmistakable edge of annoyance in her voice. "It's like an oven in here."

It wasn't, but Tyler lowered the temperature anyway. He suppressed a smile. "Do you work around here?"

Beth sank into the burgundy velvet seat, thankful for the change in subject. "I lease a suite in the medical offices building."

"You're a doctor?"

"No, but I work with them occasionally. I specialize in derma pigmentation."

"Derma what?"

"Pigmentation," Beth said with a small smile. "More commonly known as tattooing." She saw his startled look from the corner of her eye. Then she saw the car stopped directly in front of them, the car they were approaching much too fast, and her heart leaped into her throat.

"Look out!"

Tyler jerked and slammed on the brakes. Tires squalled and the big car stopped mere inches from a collision. Tyler muttered something vehement and colorful under his breath, then asked, "Are you all right?"

Her pulse was pounding at twice its normal speed and she thought she might have left imprints of her fingernails in the armrest, but yes, she was okay. She could even find the humor and gave a shaky laugh.

"At least I was wearing my seatbelt this time."

He didn't share her humor. "It's nothing to joke about, Beth. As long as you're in this car, you're my responsibility. You could have been hurt."

He had a point, but Beth felt he was over-reacting. "I appreciate your concern, but I'm fine."

She met his gaze, briefly, and saw the unguarded truth in his silver-gray eyes. It was more than simple concern for a passenger that had him reacting so strongly. Her stomach clenched. *Don't do this to me. Don't care so much.*

Traffic began moving again and Tyler kept his attention on the road. He braked at the next red light and met her gaze full force. "I'm sorry, Beth. It's just that you're not what I expected a tattoo artist to look like."

Beth pretended surprise. "And what should I look like?"

Cindy Hiday

"You know," his mouth tipped lopsidedly, "big, burly, a beard to your waist and M-O-M across your chest." When she didn't immediately deny his stereotypical description, his cocky smile wavered. "You don't have...you know..." He pressed his palm to his chest.

Beth laughed, more amused than offended. "Of course not. The light's green."

He faced forward and set the car in motion. "You do have a tattoo though?"

"Yes. Do you?"

"No."

They crossed the Willamette River, leaving the bright city center skyline behind.

"You're welcome to visit my studio sometime." Beth pulled a business card from her purse and tucked it into his lapel pocket. "I'll give you a tour."

"Where is it?"

"The address is on the card. Third floor, suite 301."

"I meant your tattoo."

Beth smiled at him. "Which one?"

"How many do you have?" he asked.

As though surprised there could be more than one, but didn't want it to show. She'd encountered that reaction before, as well.

64

Again, she laughed. "I think I'll let you worry about that for awhile."

He would, too, damn it. Although he had to admit that looking for them held a certain undeniable appeal. He glanced over at her. The hint of a smile lingered on her lush, full lips. He'd met his share of beautiful women in his line of work, but none as evocative or intriguing as this one.

He pulled into her driveway moments later and sensed something wasn't right. But he couldn't quite put his finger on what was out of place.

Beth gasped. "Santa's drowning!"

Before Tyler could ask her what she was talking about, she was out of the car and running for the corner of the porch. The downspout had come loose from the gutter and knocked the plastic Santa over. He lay on his back with his face under the steady stream of water gushing from the broken spout. How an old hunk of plastic could drown was a mystery to Tyler, but it obviously meant a lot to Beth, and she was going to drown herself trying to rescue the silly thing. He got out to help.

By the time he reached her, she'd pulled Santa under cover of the porch. Her hair lay flat against her head and water coursed down her cheeks.

She looked from the prone figure to Tyler. "I think he's dead."

"Dead?"

"His light's gone out."

The only thing that kept Tyler from laughing was the pain in her expression. He had a suspicion rain wasn't the only thing dampening her cheeks, and his heart squeezed. He didn't know where she was coming from or why, but at the moment it didn't matter.

He pulled her into his arms. "I'll fix him," he promised, not at all certain he could. But that didn't matter right now either. What did matter was comforting the woman's anguish. He held her tight and stroked her wet hair.

She clung to the front of his jacket, her head cradled against his shoulder. "It's stupid, I know, to get so emotional over an old thing like—"

"It's not stupid."

"He's been in my family for a long time."

"I figured as much."

She pulled back to look at him. The lightly veiled vulnerability in her expression was nearly his undoing.

"Do you really think you can fix him?"

"I'll try my damnedest."

He would, too, Beth realized. She could see it in his eyes. And he hadn't laughed at her. For a moment, she forgot her conviction not to become involved with this man and took pleasure in the feel of his arms around her. Strong. Comforting. Undemanding. Her gaze lowered to his mouth. How long had it been since she'd kissed a man simply because it was what she wanted? She felt herself lean into him ever so slightly, saw his head dip toward hers. His embrace changed, his broad hands moving up her back to press her closer.

Panic skittered through her and she gave an involuntary shiver.

Tyler stiffened, then took a half-step back, putting space between them, though his hands still rested lightly on her hips. "You should get out those wet things."

There was nothing suggestive or untoward in the statement. Genuine concern edged his handsome features. Beth lowered her arms, a mixture of regret and relief flooding her. Another shiver racked her body, but she knew it wasn't from the cold rain that had soaked through her trenchcoat. She'd come dangerously close to doing something she'd told herself would never happen. Had practically invited it.

And he'd been the first to back away.

"You're right." She moved from his touch and drew a ring of keys out of her pocket. Bo Diddley heard the familiar sound and gave an impatient woof from inside the house. "Okay, boy," she called through the door. "I'll be there in a second."

She inserted the key in the deadbolt. Tyler's hand closed over hers. Startled, she looked up. The intensity of his eyes made her breath catch.

"Come with me," he said.

Anywhere, she thought, then quickly recovered her senses. "Come with you? Where?"

He drew his hand back and gave her a smile that dimpled only one side of his face. "To the mall."

Beth stared at him, thinking she should understand. "The mall?"

"I promised I'd take my daughter shopping this evening. You could change into some dry clothes and come with us. We'll pick up something to eat—"

"Thank you, but I can't."

"You'd be a lot more help choosing a party dress than I would. Holly says everything I pick out is dumb. But I won't let her go to the mall alone at night, and all of her friends are busy."

Beth smiled, envisioning a harried Tyler trying to convince a budding young girl that pink ruffles were not out of style. "How old is your daughter?"

"Seventeen. Actually, she'll be eighteen in a couple more weeks. She was born on Christmas day."

Beth caught herself staring again. "I'm sorry, it's just that you don't look old enough to have a child that age."

"I'm thirty-four. And Holly isn't exactly a child anymore."

"No, of course not."

His mouth took a self-deprecating twist. "I'm having a hard time accepting the fact that my little girl will be going to college next Fall."

"It's just been the two of you?"

"Since Grandma Lou passed away seven years ago."

"It must have been hard."

"Yes," he admitted. "I know there are times when Holly could use a feminine influence in her life, but we've managed. Now, about tonight..."

Warning bells went off in Beth's head. If he was looking for a feminine influence for his daughter, he could just look somewhere else. She didn't do motherly advice. Where was the girl's real mother anyway?

"I'm sorry," she told him politely, "but my answer's still no."

Thankfully, he didn't persist or ask for an explanation. "Next time then."

Beth wanted to tell him there wouldn't be a next time, that this relationship couldn't be allowed to go any farther, but he'd already turned away. She watched as he knelt beside her plastic Santa and started tucking its cord into the cavity at the base.

Incredibly, she felt tears well in her eyes. The only reason she still had the dumb thing was because it hadn't been with the other Christmas decorations when her husband had decided to throw them all in the trash. He'd been jealous of a bunch of glass bobbles and paper angels. Ornaments that had belonged to her grandmother.

"You don't have to waste your time on that," she said, pushing her tears back and steeling herself for the inevitable.

Tyler stood and tucked Santa under his arm. "I don't consider it a waste of my time."

"Why are you doing this?" Beth asked on a sigh.

"Because, pretty lady," he stepped close and she was shocked to feel his hand tremble as he gently brushed his knuckles along her cheek, "you've done something to me and I don't seem to have a choice."

"Don't—"

"I'll be by in the morning to fix that gutter," he said, backing away.

"No."

But he appeared not have heard her as he snugged Santa more firmly into the crook of his arm and headed for his limousine.

~~~

Holly looked up from her Stephen King paperback and made a face. "Where did you get that ugly thing?"

Tyler crossed the kitchen, noted the clean dishes in the drain and plunked Santa on the table in front of his daughter. "That's no way to talk about Santa Claus."

"Dad, you're not seriously going to put that out where people can see it, are you?"

"You'll have to excuse my daughter," Tyler said, looking into the fat man's perpetually jolly, vacant face. "You have my permission to leave a lump of coal in her stocking."

"I can't talk to you when you're in one of your weird moods." Holly shook her head and buried her nose in her book again.

Tyler chuckled, not the least put out by his daughter's criticism. "Are you ready to go?"

"Is Santa coming with us?" she asked without looking up.

"Santa is going in the basement."

Holly marked her place and put her book down. "Yeah, I'm ready."

Tyler tucked Santa under his arm. "Give me a minute to put this guy away and change out of my uniform."

"Hurry. I'm starving."

Tyler smiled to himself as he flipped the switch next to the basement door, illuminating the bare bulb hanging from the ceiling, and descended the steps. One thing he'd never had to worry about was his daughter's appetite.

A damp, musty smell rose to greet him. He suspected the old concrete walls had developed a leak, but he hadn't been able to locate it yet. Or it might be the washer. It was about due for another overhaul.

He went to the long wooden workbench in the middle of the room and carefully laid Santa down. A quick glance at the blackened wires at the base of the socket told him the casing had become brittle and allowed moisture in. To be on the safe side, he'd replace both socket and cord. He made a mental note to look for what he needed at the electrical supply store in the mall.

"Don't worry, old man," he said, "I'll have you good as new in no time." He eyed Santa's faded features—the black pupils that were all but nonexistent, the once bright red suit, now pale pink—and muttered, "More or less."

He remembered Beth's tears when she'd thought she would have to throw the plastic figure out and realized what it was about her that drew him to her. There was no denying she was beautiful in a wild, illusive way. And she stirred desires that ran like an underground river through him with her voice, her laugh, her smile. But it went beyond mere physical attraction.

It was the uncertainty behind her slightly arrogant attitude. Her vulnerability. Her tears had touched him. He'd seen the edge of her caution and it was just enough to make him want more. He pulled her business card from his pocket. *Derma Definitions, by Elizabeth Heart, B.F.A.: Cosmetic and Medical Tattooing, Custom Designs.* "I'll be damned." The more he learned about the woman, the more intrigued he became. She'd tried to tell him she wasn't interested, but he hadn't imagined the look in her eyes as he'd held her. He wasn't about to walk away from something that strong, that right feeling. Her resistance only fueled his determination.

But he would have to be subtle. He'd thrown her off balance this evening when he'd pulled away. That was good. If he could keep her guessing long enough, he'd find a way to breach the wall she'd erected around her heart.

He looked at the hollow plastic figure on his hobby table. And if subtlety didn't work, he'd hold Old Saint Nick up for ransom.

4

Bo Diddley's persistent barking from the other end of the house broke into Beth's consciousness and she groggily opened her eyes. The dark gray of another cloud-choked morning filtered through the partially closed blinds at her bedroom window. Confused, she peered at the digital clock on her nightstand. Eight-o-five. She had another twenty minutes before the alarm went off.

"Darn it," she groaned. Bo knew the schedule. Why did he want out now? And why did it sound like he was at the front door when he always went out back in the morning?

Then she heard it—someone on the porch. Was that the doorknob rattling? *Oh God, somebody's trying to break into the house!* Beth's pulse raced as she leaped out of bed and hastily pulled her white terry robe on over her chemise. Hands trembling, she grabbed the baseball bat from under the bed and quietly tiptoed barefooted to the front room, weapon held high.

Bo was studying the door. He glanced back at her approach, barked once, then looked at the door again as if impatient for her to open it. His tail wagged.

Beth lowered the bat a fraction. "What...?"

The big shepherd whined and pushed at the doorknob with his nose.

Relief at realizing no one had been trying to get in came as a rush of air from Beth's lungs. But an instant later, she heard something bounce off the porch railing and a man's muffled curse. Her pulse surged. Bo began barking again.

There came a soft, "Shh," from outside the door.

To Beth's amazement, Bo quieted.

Clutching the bat tightly in her right hand, she went to the window that looked onto the porch and stealthily pushed the curtain aside.

Tyler.

Her pulse took another jolt. She found herself staring at his denim-clad butt as he bent to retrieve the screwdriver he'd apparently dropped. A metal extension ladder was propped against the side of her house. Tyler's Jeep was parked behind her Geo in the driveway. Sammy's little pickup was there as well and Beth prayed her friend was still asleep.

Beth rapped sharply on the windowpane. Tyler straightened and turned, flashing his dimpled smile at her.

"Good morning," he mouthed.

Ignoring the betraying bump of her heart against her chest, Beth frowned back at him. "What are you doing?"

He pretended not to understand, shaking his head and cupping a hand behind his ear. His smoke-gray eyes and wicked smile dared her to open the door.

Beth yanked the curtain back into place. She would open the door, all right. Leaning the bat against the small Victorian table she used for mail, keys and a vase of dusty silk flowers, she unlocked the deadbolt, nudged Bo out of the way with her knee, and jerked the door open. The cool morning air bit her heated skin. A freshness lingered like an invitation to begin a new day. It had stopped raining.

Bo pushed his way between her and the

doorjamb and went to Tyler. Beth's mouth compressed. *Some guard dog you are.*

"Good morning, fella." Scratching the shepherd between the ears, Tyler looked at Beth and her heart hummed. "Sleep well?" he asked.

No. She'd had disturbing dreams all night. Dreams of a tall man in black on a white horse. She dug her fingers into the edge of the door. "Do you realize what time it is?"

Tyler's dark brows lifted innocently. "Did I wake you?"

"Yes!"

"I'm sorry."

But he didn't look it. In fact he was looking far too interested in what she had on beneath her gaping robe. A pale rose-colored satin chemise that barely brushed the tops of her thighs. Hardly winter wear, but she preferred sleeping uninhibited by heavy knits and flannels. That's why electric blankets had been invented, as far as she was concerned.

Beth pulled her robe tightly around her and tied a thick knot in the belt. "What are you doing?" she asked again.

"Fixing your gutter."

"I distinctly remember telling you not to bother."

He grinned. He didn't seem the least bit offended by her inhospitable mood. "I must have missed that part."

Beth wasn't about to ask him what part he did remember. If it had anything to do with what had kept her tossing and turning most of the night, she didn't want to discuss it. Especially not with the man responsible. Over and over again, he'd come for her, ever nearer, his mouth inviting hers to get lost in the taste of him. But she couldn't taste in her dreams what she'd never experienced in reality. Over and over again, she'd dreamed of kissing him, only to waken an instant before their lips touched. Frustrated and hating herself for it, she'd lay in her dark room, staring at the ceiling, willing herself to go back to sleep, yet almost afraid to because she knew Tyler waited for her there.

"Look," she said, "if I've given you the impression that I can't take care of myself because of that incident with Dr. Heller—"

"Not at all."

"I'm quite capable of making my own repairs."

"I'm sure you are." His mouth settled into a smile meant to charm. "But you're too late."

"What do you mean?"

"The job's already done."

Beth gave the downspout a cursory glance. It looked good as new. "How long have you been here?"

"About half an hour." He closed his toolbox. "I'm surprised your dog didn't wake you sooner." When his gaze met hers, amusement danced in his eyes. "You must be a heavy sleeper."

Beth glared at him. It was his fault she'd finally fallen into an exhausted state of unconsciousness close to daylight. "What about my Santa?" she asked, hating the petulant tone of her voice.

"He's going to take a little longer. Got any coffee made?"

As a matter of fact, she did. She'd gotten in the habit of setting the timer on the coffee maker the night before—after having to rush to work one too many mornings without her caffeine. She could smell it brewing from here. As could Tyler, she was sure.

She gave a sigh of resignation. The man was impossible. "Help yourself. You know where the kitchen is." She turned and headed back inside. "I'm going to take a shower." She didn't wait to see whether or not he followed.

He would. Beth didn't doubt it for a second.

Leaving him to fend for himself, she gathered her clothes and shut herself in the bathroom. If nothing else, Tyler Stone was persistent, she thought, as she struggled with the knot in her robe. Remembering the appreciative look that had prompted her to tie the darn thing in the first place sent a wave of heat through her.

Unfortunately, he had a lot more going for him than just persistence, she reluctantly admitted.

The knot gave and Beth undressed. She caught a glimpse of herself in the vanity mirror and stopped. Her hair was a tangled mass and her eyelids heavy, as if sleep-drugged. But it was the odd rosiness to her skin that had her staring. It tingled, she realized, running her hand up her arm. Her breasts were taut and sensitive. When was the last time a man had had that effect on her?

She turned away from her image with an impatient grunt. The man had barged into her dreams, invaded her privacy, and was probably going through her kitchen cupboards this very moment. And she was acting like a love-struck teenager.

He hasn't even kissed you, for Heaven's sake.

Not that she wanted him to, she told herself,

annoyed that the thought had even entered her head. Adjusting the water temperature to cool, Beth climbed into the shower and scrubbed her skin until it stung.

She realized the futility of her action when she came out of the bathroom a short while later and saw Tyler sitting at the bar with his broad hands wrapped around one of her delicate Spanish Lace coffee cups. She was reminded of his tenderness the evening before, when she'd gotten so emotional over Santa Claus, the way those strong hands of his had held her, and her skin prickled with renewed awareness.

Bo Diddley had curled up at his feet, having already accepted the man's presence in their home. As if it felt right to him. *It does feel right*, Beth thought with dismay.

Tyler sensed her approach, felt her studying him. Trying to decide how to get rid of him, no doubt, he thought with a private smile. So he hadn't been all that subtle, showing up unannounced and inviting himself in. Whatever worked.

And she was flustered. He saw it in the heightened color in her cheeks when he tipped his head and looked at her. They were the same charming shade of pink her entire body had become when she'd caught him admiring her frivolous, enticing sleepwear. She was tough and independent, but she liked pretty things. He liked that about her. It had taken a great deal of willpower to keep from sweeping her off the porch then and there, and hauling her back to bed. He'd thought of little else all night.

She'd dressed in a floral print skirt that hugged her small waist and swirled at mid-calf when she moved. A scoop-necked teal cardigan revealed a dusting of freckles at her throat that veed to a point between her breasts. Soft, damp curls framed her freshly scrubbed face. The alluring, gentle fragrance of roses preceded her and Tyler breathed in deeply.

"I see you found everything all right," she said, sweeping past him and into the kitchen. The German shepherd got up and followed her.

"Yes, thank you."

She disappeared into a small pantry and came out an instant later with a huge scoop of dry dog food. Bo Diddley waited at his empty dish. Beth whispered some unintelligible endearment to him, planted a quick kiss on his muzzle and gave him his food. The big dog caught her chin with the tip of his tongue, drawing a soft laugh from her.

For one crazy second, Tyler felt jealous of his newfound four-legged friend.

Returning the scoop to the pantry, Beth proceeded to set a huge box of flaked cereal on the bar, followed by a carton of skim milk. She went to the cupboard above the microwave and pulled it open.

"Have you had breakfast?" she asked over her shoulder.

"Yes, but thanks anyway."

She took out a bowl and closed the door.

"What time do you have to leave for work?" Tyler asked.

She got a spoon from the dishwasher, then poured herself a cup of coffee and brought everything to the bar. "I have to catch the bus by nine-twenty," she said. She rested her bottom on the edge of the stool next to his. "I open the studio at ten."

"Can I—"

"No." She reached for the box of cereal. "I am taking the bus."

Tyler decided not to push it. In all honesty, he didn't have time to take her downtown and still make his first appointment. "So tell me, where'd your interest in tattooing come from?"

His question surprised her enough that she

poured cereal on the counter. Quickly sweeping the flakes into the palm of her hand and depositing them in her bowl, she answered, "You wouldn't believe me if I told you."

"Try me."

She tossed him a brief glance as if to see whether or not he was serious, then reached for the milk. "All right. When I was nine, my dad took me to the circus and—"

"You saw the painted lady."

Beth smiled and added milk to her cereal.

"You're kidding."

She set the carton down and picked up her spoon. "I knew you wouldn't believe me."

"How did you get your dad to agree to such a thing?"

"I could be very stubborn," she said around a mouthful of cereal.

Tyler resisted the impulse to point out that she still was. Instead, he simply smiled and said, "Go on."

"Well, my poor dad had to literally drag me away. Oh, I'd seen small tattoos before, and embarrassed my parents by staring shamelessly, but nothing like the painted lady. The idea of using the human body as a pallet for artistic expression fascinated me."

Tyler sat captivated, not only by the fact that she was being so open with him, but she had a way of eating and talking at the same time that he'd thought only his daughter had mastered.

"Anyway, after that, I begged Mom and Dad to let me get a tattoo. Of course they refused." She took another bite.

"What did you do?"

"I took felt-tipped markers and did it myself. By the time my mom discovered what I was doing, I'd illustrated my arms and legs and had started on my belly." Beth's mouth quirked. "Of course I used permanent ink."

Tyler gave a wry smile. "Is there any other kind?" He remembered trying to wash permanent marker off Grandma Lou's dining room wall during one of Holly's artistic moments.

"It was the middle of summer and I had to wear long pants and long-sleeved shirts until my artwork had finally faded enough for Mom to let me show myself in public."

"When did you get your first real tattoo?"

"Prom night. On a dare. I thought my date was going to faint."

"Did he get one, too?"

She almost choked on her cereal. "Good Lord, no! I never saw Mr. Future Ivy League again after that."

Tyler smiled, unexplainably pleased. "What kind of tattoo did you get?"

"A heart."

"Of course. What did your folks have to say about it?"

"They didn't find out until a month later, when I made the mistake of wearing my bikini in front of them." She shot him a slightly wicked smile that made the blood race through his veins. "I think that's when Dad realized how serious I was about tattooing. He was a plastic surgeon, you know." She shoveled more cereal into her mouth. "He began studying the possibilities of utilizing the art in his own practice, using tattooing to hide scar tissue, blend skin tones, reconstruct disfigurements." Her expression softened, became distant. "He had it all figured out, how one day the two of us would work side by side."

"And did you?"

The pain of a buried memory etched her features. "He died before we got the chance."

"I'm sorry, Elizabeth. I know what it's like to lose someone you're close to."

"It happened five years ago. Shortly before..." Her voice trailed off.

"What?" Tyler gently coaxed.

Cindy Hiday

"It's not important." She stood and carried her dirty dishes to the sink. "Mom still lives in Seattle," she told him, speaking over the running water. She shut off the tap and dried her hands. "Oh, she sold the big old house they'd lived in and bought a condo, but she said she could never leave the city where she and Dad had fallen in love."

"But you left."

Another memory marred her face, this one full of bitterness. "I needed a change of scenery." She turned to take his empty coffee cup to the sink.

"How long has it been since you've seen your mother?"

"She comes down every summer for a month."

"But you've never been back to Seattle?"

"No."

She'd shut him out again. But Tyler was beginning to realize he could learn as much from her silences as he could from getting her to talk about herself. Whatever it was she was hiding from him, it had hurt her deeply. The scars were still there, just below the surface. He ached to know what, or who, had done this to her, had caused her to pull inside herself.

But it was going to take tenderness and

patience. A lot of it. He stood and carefully stepped over Bo Diddley. "I've got to go. Thanks again for the coffee."

"Tyler?" She turned and looked at him.

"Hmm?"

A hesitant smile curved her mouth. "Thank you for fixing the gutter."

"You're welcome." He thrust his hands in the pockets of his jeans. "I couldn't help noticing the way your mailbox leans."

"Sammy backed over it with her pickup."

"I'll come by tomorrow morning and straighten it for you."

Her smile faded. "I wish you wouldn't."

Tyler heard the unmistakable edge of desperation in her voice. He wished to God he knew what was going on in that pretty head of hers. What was she afraid of?

"Is this your independent streak talking again?" he ventured softly. "Or are you telling me you don't want to see me?"

She hugged her arms around her middle. "I don't want to feel obligated to you."

He knew that. What he didn't know was why. "I told you before, I'm doing this because I want to. I don't expect anything in return."

"Yes," she quietly accused, "you do."

She was right. Tyler felt like he was treading

through a minefield as he moved to the end of the bar, then closer, until he stood an arm's length from her. Her eyes grew large. Wary. But she didn't back away. "I like being with you. Is that so bad?"

"It depends on what you hope to gain." She brought her chin up. "If you're looking for something long-term—"

"A kiss."

"W-what?"

He nearly smiled at her charming, flustered reaction. "You asked me what I hoped to gain. Well, I'm telling you."

"You're not making any sense."

"Then let me explain." He closed the remaining distance between them. In the bright florescent lighting, he noticed for the first time that her green eyes had tiny flecks of brown scattered through them. She stared at him like a cornered doe, but he knew better. He'd seen what she was capable of when she felt trapped. No, it was something else making her look at him that way, something he could only guess at.

"I want to know if your lips taste as sweet as they look," he told her, his voice low.

There, just for an instant, so fleeting he would have missed it had he blinked, desire flickered in her cat-like eyes. The color over her high cheekbones deepened. The dull ache in Tyler's gut became a sharp, focused need to possess.

"I..." She worried her lower lip between her perfect white teeth. "That's all?"

Hell no! One kiss wouldn't begin to satisfy the need he had for her. Her gentleness. Her fight. Her passion. He wanted it all. She remained perfectly still as he brought his hand up to trace the delicate line of her jaw with his thumb, his fingers finding their way beneath the silken, still-damp hair at her nape.

Tipping her head back, he swept his lips over hers and whispered, "For now."

Beth held her breath as his lips hovered, lightly brushing hers without making solid contact. Vaguely, she was aware that he might be giving her time to tell him no.

It was too late. She was old enough to know he wouldn't settle for just one kiss, old enough to know better than to play with fire. But the match had already been struck. When his warm mouth met hers, her arms were already finding their way up his back. She was already leaning into him, the flames he'd ignited licking through her entire body.

He wasn't a soft man. Her fingers kneaded

taut muscles beneath his flannel shirt, the thighs that pressed against hers lean and ungiving. But it was his mouth, coaxing, teasing, inviting, that stole the breath from her lungs. When was the last time a man had dared to kiss her like that? When was the last time she'd wanted a man to kiss her like that? Like he wanted her. Needed her.

Too long.

He slid his hand from her nape to the back of her head, burying his fingers in her hair and holding her there to deepen the kiss. His other made its way slowly, languorously, to the base of her spine and applied gentle pressure.

It was a subtle move that sent what little breath she had left rushing from her in a soft whoosh. She thought of pulling away, thought it would be best if she did, but couldn't quite. Not because of the way he held her, but because her legs had gone weak and the room was spinning.

And she was still hungry.

Sinking her fingers into his hard back, she chased his seeking tongue with her own, tasted him the way he tasted her.

A tortured groan rose in his chest, became her name, spoken as a muffled breath against her lips. The fingers in her hair tightened and the pressure at the small of her back increased, making her aware of what she was doing to him, the evidence hard against her abdomen. A coil of desire, so strong it stunned her, sent a tremor through her.

What was happening to her? Where was her self-control? "Tyler..."

The soft plea in her voice broke through the heavy pounding of Tyler's heart. He eased his hold on her, moving his arms to embrace her as he dropped his head back and sucked in deep breaths. He'd been kissed by women before, but never devoured.

He looked at her, saw the confusion in her flecked eyes, the passion that lingered there. He gently smoothed her hair back from her heart-shaped face. "What are you doing to me, pretty lady?"

Her red, kiss-crushed lips parted. "I don't—"

"Knock, knock!" a female voice called lustily from the front room. Bo Diddley jumped to his feet and woofed. It was answered by a quick laugh. "Good morning to you, too, big guy! Bethie, are you—oops."

A young woman with short auburn hair, gelled into a spiky style, came around the corner, stopped short and eyed Tyler with intense interest. A broad smile curled the corners of her mouth. "So," she said, folding her arms across the front of her bulky black sweater, her legs, clad in white Spandex, braced as though it would take a tank to make her move, "I finally get to meet the limo driver."

Tyler felt Beth stiffen an instant before she pulled out of his arms. She was embarrassed and it annoyed her, he realized, judging by her flushed cheeks and the frown that drew her arched brows together. But who the target of that annoyance was, he couldn't be sure.

Her glance skimmed off his and stopped somewhere between the woman and him. "Tyler—" Her voice squeaked and the color in her cheeks deepened. She cleared her throat and tried again. "Tyler, this is Samantha Dixon, the friend I told you about."

He met the young woman's unabashedly steady gaze. "It's a pleasure, Samantha."

"Call me Sam, please. And the pleasure's all mine."

"Sam and I take the bus in together," Beth explained.

"Which we're going to miss if we don't get a move on." Sam gave Tyler an apologetic look. "Sorry."

Tyler smiled. "I was just leaving." He met

Beth's gaze and his smile tipped. She looked delectably mussed, like a woman who'd just been thoroughly kissed and wasn't quite sure what to do about it. Good.

He wanted to touch her, one last stroke of her cheek, but decided against it. "I'll see you in the morning," he promised and turned away.

"Wait a minute," she said, irritation evident in her voice.

But he didn't. He wasn't going to give her the chance to tell him no again. Not that he would have listened any better than he had the first time. With determined steps, he walked out of the house and climbed into his Jeep.

Beth listened to Tyler drive away. He'd done it again, she thought. Made her babble. Made her want. For a few brief moments, he'd made her forget. And she'd invited it. She'd let a moment's impulse cloud her judgment.

Dear Lord, she'd let him kiss her.

She touched her fingers to her lips, certain they were still on fire. He hadn't simply kissed her. He'd *branded* her.

"You all right?" Sam asked.

Beth started, looked at her friend. "I don't think so."

5

Flames, so close she could feel them lick her body with their hot talons, red and gold, leaping higher and higher into the dark, starless sky. She tried to back away, but her feet refused to move. She tried to scream, but could do no more than moan, mute with terror. Frantically, she strained to see through the fire.

There. A break in the wall of heat. And a man, tall and blond and handsomely dressed. He would help her. But as he turned and looked at her, a tremor clawed its way up her back. His eyes were hard and empty of feeling. Evil. She drew away in fear. The flames encircled her.

Hot. So hot. She shrank from the pain, felt the sweat roll down her face, her arms, the middle of her back. Again, she opened her mouth to scream, but no sound could be forced from her scorched lungs.

A white shape appeared and she believed it to be the end—the bright light of death. She watched it, transfixed, and realized it was coming toward her. Taking form. A horse. Massive and powerful. The muscles in its legs and neck bunched and stretched in its charge toward her. It reached the outer edges of the fire's glare and she saw the man astride, a man in black, a shadow riding low over his mount's thick neck, his long legs gripping the beast's heaving sides, his fingers buried in the noble white mane whipping at his face.

Dear God, they're going to trample me to death! But as beast and rider leaped through the flames, she saw the man's eyes and the terror in her heart stilled. They were the color of smoke. Passion burned in them. They locked with hers and she realized he'd come for her. She was the reason for his passion. She was the reason he would charge into an inferno without a second's hesitation. He reached his arm to her and she took it. The horse barely broke stride as she was swept onto its broad bare back with one mighty pull.

"Hold on," the man in black ordered, his voice deep and disturbingly sensual.

She wrapped her arms around his taut waist and pressed her face into the corded muscles of his back. His shirt was damp. He too had been affected by the *heat of the fire that swirled around them. The thought comforted her. He was human. Flesh and blood to her flesh and blood. His heart beat hard and heavy beneath her cheek. Then once again their mount leapt and she felt the flames make one last grab at her ankles. She closed her eyes and waited for the abrupt jolt of the horse's hooves striking earth, but seconds stretched into minutes, and still they climbed. The air cooled.*

She opened her eyes and was amazed to find the horse had sprouted massive flame-colored wings. Crimson. Bright gold. Beneath her, muscles and mane became feathers and talons and suddenly she and the man were no longer riding a horse at all, but a huge eagle-like bird with a purple hood.

A phoenix.

The man's deep, rich laughter rumbled through him and filled the night. He twisted in her arms to look at her.

"Did you think it would be any other way?" he asked.

She could only stare at him, mesmerized, entranced by the smoky depths of his eyes. As if he and the fire had become one. She felt his heat reach out to her, envelope her, his flames a torture much more devastating. She felt herself being consumed by a longing, a need so deep it drummed through her. A primitive rhythm...

"Good morning! The time is 8:25 and that was Chris Isaak singing *In the Heat of the Jungle*. I'm—"

Beth sat bolt upright in bed and slapped at the radio alarm, cutting the DJ off in mid sentence. A chill wracked her sweat-drenched body in the sudden silence. She clutched the rose-pink bedcovers to her breasts and struggled to clear the dream that remained vivid in her head.

Tyler, her rescuer. Her knight on a white horse. But why had she felt the need to be rescued from a man she'd fled four years ago? Why had that part of her past come back to haunt her now? The terrible loss of identity, the overwhelming sense of powerlessness, her shattered self-esteem. It all came charging forward, sending another wracking chill through her.

It can't hurt you anymore. He *can't hurt you.*

But the feeling of impending tumult wouldn't release her.

Shaken, Beth slipped into her robe and went to the living room. Bo Diddley had curled up in front of the door. He opened one eye and peered at her with that patient, self-sacrificing look he used to make her feel guilty for one thing or another. This time it was because she'd kept him waiting to be let out.

She pulled back the curtain, already knowing what she would see. Still, her heart bumped hard against her chest. The Jeep was parked behind her little red car as if it belonged there. And beyond it, at the end of the drive, Tyler shoveled dirt around the base of the mailbox post he'd reset.

It was a cloudless morning. Dew glistened on the grass and dripped from the tips of the fir tree at the side of the house. Tyler had taken off his heavy flannel shirt and hung it over the Jeep's side mirror to work in his T-shirt. A black T-shirt. Beth wondered if she were to go to him and press her face to his back, would it be damp with the heat of his sweat? Would his heart beat hard and heavy beneath her cheek?

A hot ache coiled through her and she lowered the curtain. It was just a dream, she told herself.

Then why do I feel scorched?

She unlocked the door and let Bo out, then went to take another cool shower. When she re-emerged a short while later, feeling confident in a conservative delft-blue knit dress that started high on her neck, tucked at the waist, then flared to a full skirt that reached the tops of her ankle-high boots, Tyler was in the kitchen setting out toast and a platter of scrambled eggs. He'd donned a gaudy sunflower-print apron she'd forgotten she even owned.

And he'd fed Bo Diddley.

Beth sat at the bar, speechless.

"I hope you don't mind," he said, putting a plate in front of her. "I thought you might enjoy a break from cold cereal."

Beth's stomach gave a betraying rumble. "Where did you find the eggs?"

"I picked them up on my way over." Tyler scooped some onto her plate, not giving her an opportunity to protest. He'd laid awake last night planning this little scheme, not at all sure how she would react. But he'd decided it was worth a shot. There was more than one way to charm a woman. Especially one who didn't cook. He watched the play of expressions on her face. It was as though she wasn't sure what her reaction should be either.

To his mild surprise, she picked up her fork and quietly began eating. Tyler suppressed the smile of satisfaction that tugged at his mouth.

"Am I in the right house?" he heard Sam question loudly from the front room. "I actually smell food cooking." She whirled into the kitchen in a florescent lime-green blouse and snug black skirt, the tips of her spiky auburn hair tinted orange. She took in the homey scene with a wide-eyed sweep that stopped on Tyler. "Hi, handsome."

Tyler returned her smile, grateful for her easygoing acceptance of him. It occurred to him he might have an ally in Beth's friend. "Good morning. Have you eaten?"

"You did this?" Sam took a seat at the bar and Tyler put a plate in front of her. "I'm impressed."

"I thought you didn't do breakfast," Beth said around a mouthful of toast.

"I can make an exception." Sam grinned.

Tyler watched the silent exchange, the warning in the look Beth gave her friend, and the casual way her friend chose to ignore it. Yes, he would have to get to know Samantha Dixon better. He went to the sink to wash out the skillet.

"You're not eating?" Beth asked him.

"I had breakfast with Holly."

"Thanks for fixing the mailbox," Sam piped in between bites. "Now I won't have to listen to any more wisecracks about how the postman has to stand on his head to leave the mail."

Tyler looked over in time to see Beth shoot another killing look in Sam's direction. His smile broadened. "You're welcome."

"You know," Sam said, pointing at him with a forkful of egg, "I believe I could get used to having you aro—"

"We've got a bus to catch." Beth abruptly put her fork down and stood. She took her plate to the sink and collided with Tyler.

"I'll get those," he told her.

"No, I will."

They stared at each other, neither yielding. Beth's flecked green eyes snapped. Even in anger, she's gorgeous, Tyler thought. He wanted to kiss her, there in front of Sam and Bo and the whole damn world. The memory of the kiss they'd shared yesterday, the sweetness and heat of her mouth on his, had plagued him for the past twenty-four hours. His desire must have shown in his face, because her brows suddenly arched and she drew in a soft gasp through her parted lips. She knew he wanted to kiss her, wanted it herself, if he was reading her right.

And it terrified her.

That alone was enough to make him clamp down on the dull ache, like an unsatisfied craving, that drummed through him. He wanted to confuse her, rattle her composure, not scare her off.

"Why is it you don't drive to work?" he asked, changing tactics.

"There's nothing wrong with my car," she said with a sudden flash of amusement in her expression, "if you're looking for something else to fix."

Tyler chuckled and stepped aside so she could get to the sink. "That's not why I asked."

"The bus lets us off a block from the medical building." She turned on the water and rinsed her plate. "The parking garage is four blocks away and charges a ridiculous price."

"You could always bring your limousine by tomorrow morning," Sam suggested, a teasing glint in her hazel eyes, "and give us a ride."

"No he couldn't." The sharpness of Beth's retort had Tyler and Sam both staring at her. She swallowed nervously, her gaze darting from her friend to him. "That is, I'm sure you have better things to do with your time."

Tyler held her look just long enough to bring a flush to her cheeks. "As a matter of fact, I do have an early appointment tomorrow."

"Oh." Then realizing she'd allowed her disappointment to show, she frowned and looked away. "That's nice," she said, drying her hands as if it took all her concentration.

Tyler smiled to himself and left her standing

at the sink. He caught Sam's look. The young woman winked at him.

"Bye, handsome."

He grinned and returned the wink. "Bye."

~~~

Beth moved to the front of the bus as it approached her stop, and saw the long white limousine, sleek and gleaming in the yellow cast of the street lamp, at the curb in front of her house a block and a half away. A shiver of excitement shot through her, then annoyance. She'd missed him, dammit. The house had felt empty this morning, the bowl of cold cereal she usually inhaled without a second thought tasteless and boring. Bo had paced at the front door and whined. When she'd finally relented and let him out, he'd sniffed his way to the end of the drive, then sat, waiting. Beth had had to practically drag him back inside when it came time to leave for work.

She hadn't asked for this intrusion into the safe, secure life she'd made for herself. She didn't want to come to rely on a man's presence in that life. Nor did she want her dog to. She had a house, a car, a fulfilling career. She didn't want someone throwing the whole thing out of balance.

And yet, that was exactly how she felt. As if

her equilibrium had been knocked off kilter. She'd spent another sleep-tossed night dreaming about him, about the passion in his face as he rescued her, the way his deep laugh and sensual mouth seduced her. She'd wakened with a longing she didn't want to acknowledge.

The bus stopped and the doors opened. Beth stumbled and caught herself.

"Watch your step, Miss Heart," the driver cautioned.

Wise advise, Beth thought. She would definitely have to watch her step around Tyler Stone. She'd let her emotions make her decisions once before, with disastrous results.

She shot the bus driver a quick smile. "Thank you, Mr. Johnson. Good night."

Tyler heard the bus stop down the street, saw it drive past the house a moment later, then saw Beth skirt the juniper bush that edged her property and come up the walk toward him. His body throbbed with a need so strong he nearly groaned. He'd made himself stay away for thirty-six hours, hoping she would miss him, hoping that when he called on her again, she'd be happy to see him.

It had stopped raining for the moment and her fiery hair flew loose and free about her face in the sporadic evening breeze. Her tan trenchcoat hung open and she walked with a lithe, purposeful stride, her shapely calves tantalizing as they flashed beneath the hem of a plum-colored knee-length skirt. She glanced up at where he sat on the wide porch railing and her step faltered. But her expression was unreadable in the shadow of the street lamp behind her.

When she moved into the twinkling rainbow of lights that trimmed the front of her house, she saw Santa standing guard beside the porch steps and gave an unguarded cry of joy.

"You fixed him!"

Her eyes sparkled as they met Tyler's, the warmth in them sending his pulse racing. She looked like a child who'd just discovered exactly what she'd asked for under the Christmas tree. It made him feel incredibly good to be the one to do that for her. He hadn't had the heart to hold Saint Nick up for ransom, not when the old guy meant so much to her.

"I said I would," he told her, his voice oddly hoarse.

"You said you would try," she corrected with a teasing laugh.

"With a teenager in the house, I've learned

not to make promises I might not be able to keep."

She smiled, but he saw the retreat in her eyes. She was pulling back into that place where no one could touch her again, and it was all Tyler could do to keep from shouting his frustration. He never knew when to expect it, or what caused it.

She came up the porch steps and Bo Diddley woofed from inside the house. "I'll be there in a minute," she quieted through the closed door. Then she looked at Tyler. "I appreciate your honesty," she said. "And thank you."

"It was my pleasure."

She nodded toward the white paper bag on the railing beside him. Steam rose from its contents, spicy and tantalizing. "What's that?"

"Dinner. You do like honey roasted chicken and barbecued ribs, don't you?"

Her stomach rumbled and she gave a resigned laugh. "Yes."

"I noticed your cupboards were a little bare yesterday."

Her smiled stiffened. "I haven't had time to get groceries." She turned away and began digging through her purse.

Tyler had noticed more than her lack of stocked cupboards. The woman was exhausted. The little makeup she normally wore was gone, revealing pale cheeks and shadows beneath her eyes. But he had a feeling exhaustion wasn't the cause of her defensiveness. He stood and touched the sleeve of her coat, making her look at him. He was stunned by the raw torment in her expression.

"It wasn't meant as a criticism, Beth." He ventured a lopsided smile. "Actually, I was using it as an excuse."

Her eyes searched his face. "To have dinner with me," she said.

"I have an hour before I have to pick up my next client."

A heartbeat passed. Then slowly, her mouth curved upward. "Come in."

Beth greeted Bo, then shed her coat and purse and tossed them onto the end of the couch as she made her way to the kitchen. She grabbed plates and utensils while Tyler arranged the boxes of take-out on the bar. Barbecued ribs. Sweet roasted chicken. Mashed potatoes, mushroom gravy and coleslaw.

"Does anything need to be reheated?" Beth asked.

Tyler looked up and met the delectable sway of her hips as she reached for something on a top shelf. She balanced on her toes, her legs stretched to their full length. Her white silk blouse pulled taut against her slender, arched back, causing her bottom to curve toward him slightly. Tantalizingly. He thought of offering to help, but couldn't quite tear his eyes away from the view. He found himself wondering where exactly on her lovely body was the heart tattoo that only a bikini line would reveal.

"Tyler?"

He blinked just as she turned and gave him a questioning look, a long-stemmed wine goblet in each hand.

"Ah—" His fogged brain scrambled to remember what the question had been. "No." He popped one of the boxes open. "Nope, everything is still pretty hot." Including me.

Keep it up, Stone, and you could find yourself with a bloody nose like good old Heller.

"I have red wine, apple juice and ice water," she said, apparently oblivious to his dilemma.

"Ice water's fine." *Just throw it on me.*

Of course she didn't. She brought a goblet of water and one half-filled with a deep burgundy wine to the bar and set them next to their plates without spilling a drop.

"Am I forgetting anything?" she asked.

"Napkins." Tyler removed his uniform jacket and folded it over the back of one of the barstools. He grinned at her. "Lots of 'em."

She laughed, a light, merry sound that went straight to his heart. "Gotcha."

Moments later, they were sitting next to each other, napkins tucked into their collars, sleeves rolled, buried to their elbows in barbecue sauce and honey. Tyler smiled at the small sounds of contentment that came from Beth each time she sampled a new flavor. She and his daughter had one thing in common at least, he mused. Hearty appetites.

Beth caught him watching her out of the corner of her eye and stopped, a dripping rib half-way to her mouth. "What?" she asked with a small frown. "Do I have something 'on my face?"

"No," he said, although she did. A tiny spot of barbecue sauce dotted the point of her chin. He hoped she would forgive him for not telling her, but she looked so damned endearing. "I'm just happy you're enjoying yourself."

Her expression relaxed. "I am. This was really nice of you, Tyler."

"My intentions were purely selfish, I assure you." He chuckled at the startled look that widened her eyes. "I hate to eat alone."

"What about your daughter?"

"She's having dinner with a friend."

Beth plucked another rib from one of the boxes. "Well, all I can say is she doesn't know what she's missing."

"Speaking of friends, where's Sam?"

"She goes straight from the studio to the club."

"The club?"

"Mmm," Beth licked at a drop of barbecue sauce running down her thumb. "She moonlights as a bouncer at Juliet's. Have you heard of it?"

"It's a popular singles' hangout. I have a couple of clients who go there on a regular basis. Is that where you and Sam met?"

Beth slowly laid the remains of the rib she'd been eating on her plate. "Why do you ask?"

The wall came up so fast, Tyler could swear he heard it slam. His jaw tightened. "I thought you might have gotten your self-defense lessons from her, that's all."

"As a matter of fact, I did."

"Why do you do that, Beth? Why do you shut me out over an innocent question?"

She stared at him. "I didn't realize..." But her voice trailed off. She looked down at her plate. "There was a time when I was criticized for my choice of friends."

"By someone you were close to?"

"I thought so at the time."

"But not anymore?"

"No." Clipped and succinct.

End of subject. He asked anyway. "How long were you married?"

"Five years."

"Do you want to talk about it?"

"No." He saw the edge of desperation in her face. "It's history."

"Are you sure, Elizabeth?"

A week ago she wouldn't have had to think about her answer. Now she hesitated, and that troubled her. Her ex-husband had haunted her dreams for four nights straight. Tyler had been there, too. Beth tipped her head to study the handsome planes of his face, his strong jaw, the almost boyish angle of his nose. But there was nothing boyish or innocent in those steel-gray eyes. He saw too much with them. She felt exposed when he looked at her. She'd seen his passion, tasted it.

He'd gotten to her tonight. He'd penetrated her defenses with his charm and tenderness.

And food, darn it.

She looked away. "I'm positive," she said, then stood and began collecting the dirty dishes. "I'll take care of these. I wouldn't want you to be late for your appointment."

Tyler swiveled on the barstool, quietly took the plates from her and set them back on the bar, then pulled her toward him with a gentle tug on her wrist. She found herself standing between his splayed legs, her face level with his. She couldn't have looked away if she'd wanted to.

Which she didn't.

"I have a few minutes yet," he told her.

"I don't think this is a good idea," she said on a sigh. A tantalizing blend of spice with woodsy undertones teased her heightened senses. It's only physical, she tried telling herself as his arms gently encircled her waist. She hadn't been this close to a man in a very long time. That was the only explanation for the muzzy, boneless feeling coming over her, making her lean into his warmth, like a cocoon, wrapping her in the safety of his embrace.

As if of their own volition, her arms went around his neck.

"I don't know," he murmured, his warm breath brushing her face, "it feels pretty good to me."

"You know what I mean."

"Explain it to me."

"We have nothing in common."

"We both like sugar cookies." He pressed his lips to the point of her chin, tasting her. "And Romo's takeout."

She tried her darnedest not to smile. "That's not much to go on."

"It's a start."

She caught the shameless slant of his mouth an instant before he dipped his head and pressed that incorrigible smile to the junction of her throat and collarbone. A shiver rippled through her.

"You're moving too fast," she tried to tell him, but it came out as a breathless whisper. He was stealing the breath from her.

"Lady, I'm just getting warmed up."

"I—"

But he didn't give her a chance to explain. Not that she could have even remembered her own name, much less what she'd been about to say, when his mouth covered hers. He moved his head, parting her lips, seeking a deeper intimacy. With a small moan, Beth allowed him in, welcomed him, as the final shred of her defenses fell away.

His hands cupped her bottom and drew her deeper into the saddle of his legs. She became intensely aware of the differences between his body and hers, his heat seeping through her like a drug. *Oh, Lord, I'm lost,* she thought, and clung to him. It suddenly didn't seem to matter that she didn't know much about this man. She wanted him, bad.

When he finally pulled back, his breath was uneven, his eyes pinpoints of smoke. Stunned, Beth could only watch as he took her hand and pressed it to his chest. His heart pounded hard and fast beneath her palm.

"This is what you do to me," he said, his voice a low rasp.

"That's not possible." Her fingers curled into his shirt. "You don't even know me." Her denial rang hollow in her ears. This from a woman who'd considered making love with him just seconds ago?

"I know enough."

No, you don't. He couldn't have any idea what scared her, what made her avoid any kind of meaningful relationship with a man. She pulled out of his embrace and turned away, hugging herself.

"I'm not what you need, Tyler."

She heard him push up from the barstool, felt him move to stand behind her. "What is it you think I need?" he asked softly.

His scent caressed her. She shook her head,

unable to answer.

"Look at me, Beth. Please."

She turned, lifted her chin until her gaze met his. Though *collided* might have been a better word for the impact his pale gray eyes had on her. They drew her in, made her aware of only him.

"Do you want to see me again?" he asked.

"I—"

"Yes or no. Do you want to see me again?"

She swallowed against the cotton that seemed to be lodged in her throat. She knew it wasn't wise to continue this, whatever this was. It was too dangerous. But she couldn't lie to herself. She did want to see him again. For however long it lasted, she couldn't deny herself that much.

"Yes," she breathed.

He flashed her a dimpled smile. "Good." He grabbed his jacket and slung it over his shoulder. "I'll call you."

And then he was gone, leaving her staring at the empty entryway, again, and wondering when in the hell the man had invented fire.

6

Beth looked up from the tattoo designs she'd been re-filing when Marie poked her blonde head around the door.

"If you don't have anything more for me, boss, I'm going to call it a day."

"That's fine," Beth replied with a tired smile. "Have a good evening."

"Will do." Marie hesitated. "Tyler Stone called again this afternoon." There was the slightest hint of accusation in her associate's pursed expression. "That makes three messages he's left since Friday."

Not counting the two on my answering machine at home, Beth thought guiltily. She'd spent the weekend praying the phone wouldn't ring and jumping out of her skin when it did. She'd found reasons to be out of the house as much as possible, even going so far as to shop for groceries.

"Thank you, Marie," she said, and returned to her filing. "I'll take care of it."

She heard Marie's heavy sigh. "Well, then...goodbye."

Beth shot her a quick half-smile. "See you tomorrow."

No sooner had Marie left, than Sam came in. "You haven't returned any of his calls, have you?" She adopted Marie's accusing look.

Beth's mouth tightened and she glanced away. "No."

"Why?"

"I've been busy."

"Baloney." Sam's abrupt remark brought Beth's head up, her eyes coming to rest on the challenge in her friend's expression. "This guy's a doll, Bethie. And he can cook!"

"If you're so impressed by him, maybe you should—"

"Don't even think it." Sam folded her arms across her chest. "You know he isn't my type."

"You mean his hair's too short and he doesn't own a motorcycle," Beth said dryly.

"Hey, a girl's gotta set some guidelines. Besides, Tyler's too old for me."

"Gee thanks."

Sam shook her head. "Bethie, you can't keep doing this to yourself."

Beth looked away. "I don't know what you're talking about."

"Maybe you can lie to yourself," Sam's tone had gone cool, "but don't try it on me."

Again, guilt stabbed at Beth. With a resigned sigh, she met her friend's gaze. "I'm sorry, Sammy." She fought back the anxiety that had had her stomach so tight for the past three days—since she'd last seen Tyler, to be precise—she'd barely been able to eat. "I'm just not sure seeing him again is the right thing to do."

"Why? Has he done something to turn you off?"

Beth barely contained the desperate sound that rose in her throat. *Not hardly. That's the problem.*

"He scares me," she admitted.

"Girl, I know you had a bum marriage." Sam put a comforting arm around her shoulders. "I know that jerk, Eric what's-his-name, hurt you. But it's not fair to judge all guys by one man's jerkiness."

Despite the turmoil that tore at her, Beth laughed. "Jerkiness?"

"You know what I mean."

Unfortunately, she did. "How can I know for sure Tyler won't change on me the way Eric did?"

"You can't," her friend answered bluntly. "There are no guarantees in life, Bethie. I'm not saying rush out and marry the guy. But give him a chance. He's nice. Let yourself have some fun for once." She tipped her head closer and whispered an urgent, "Call him."

Beth's heart took a little lurch. *What would I say? How would I explain my reasons for not calling sooner?*

Sam's arm tightened around her shoulders in a quick hug before she pulled away. "I gotta run. Catch you later?"

"Sure. Thanks, Sammy."

Sam wiggled her fingers over her shoulder as she left. Beth waited until she heard the outer office door close before releasing a long, thoughtful breath.

There are no guarantees, Bethie. Let yourself have some fun.

Despair returned like a fist in her stomach. If she could just believe it were that easy.

Sam was the only one she'd ever told the details of her marriage to. And then it was only because Sam had been trying to show her how to make margaritas. They'd stayed up most of the night tasting various Tequila concoctions and pouring out their souls. Sam had never revealed a word of the secrets Beth had shared with her to anyone else. At first Beth had thought, because of the fifth they'd polished off, her young friend didn't remember most of what had been said. But she'd quickly come to realize Sam could drink the best of them under the table, as the saying went, and still recite the evening's conversation word for word.

No, Samantha Dixon was one of those rare people you could trust with your innermost thoughts, without fear of having those thoughts broadcast to half the city. Beth just wished her friend wouldn't try so hard to fix something that wasn't broken.

Wasn't it? a little voice nagged.

Perturbed, Beth shoved the cabinet drawer closed and went to her work station to re-organize the bottles of pigment she'd used that day. She usually enjoyed these moments alone in the studio, taking time to relax and reflect. It filled her with a sense of gratification to be able to look around her and know that all of this was hers and that she'd achieved a lifelong dream.

She'd come so close to losing it. All those

years she'd devoted to helping Eric succeed in the family investment firm, putting her own ambitions on hold, only to discover that no matter how much she did, it was never enough.

A sound at the door made her look up. She gave a small gasp and almost dropped the bottle of cyan pigment in her hand.

"What are you doing here?" she asked, her voice barely audible over the sudden mad drumming of her pulse in her ears.

In his black chauffeur's suit, he was a stark silhouette against the bright lights of the office behind him. His tall frame filled the doorway. His garrison cap shadowed his face, making it impossible for Beth to see his expression.

"I'm here for that tour," he said, the accusation in his deep voice clear enough.

Beth forced a calm she didn't feel. "This isn't a good time. I was just closing up."

"Let me guess," he stepped into the room, dominating it with his presence, "I should call first?"

Beth turned away, carefully set the bottle down, and said the first thing that came to mind, hoping it would fool him better than it had Sammy. "I've been very busy."

Tyler didn't answer.

He wasn't sure of his next move. His coming here had been an act of impulse. He'd dropped Mrs. Peterson off for the evening and was driving past the building when something had compelled him to park. He'd sat outside for long minutes, restarting the limousine's engine twice, before finally putting the keys in his pocket and coming inside.

Her studio wasn't what he'd expected. It looked more like a small gallery, with colors that were easy on the eyes, soft music and framed poster-size prints of stunning body art on every wall. In the center of the room was a dentist-style chair, and behind it, a long counter with bottles and instruments neatly arranged next to a stainless steel sink. Comfortable and professional, Tyler thought briefly, his gaze settling once more on Beth.

She'd gone to a small closet in the corner, next to a full-length mirror, and was removing her lab coat, her back to him. Her mid-length blue-denim skirt was split part way up the back and Tyler caught a glimpse of her calves above her ankle-high, black leather boots. An indefinable restlessness stirred in him. He didn't understand the pull he had toward this woman, what made her different from any of the others. He only knew he was unable to ignore it.

The lab coat slipped from her shoulders. She wore a silky pink camisole with thin straps. Tyler saw it immediately, the tattoo that started at the base of her neck, swept across her right shoulderblade and disappeared beneath her blouse. Curiosity drew him closer.

It was a bird with an eagle-like body, its crimson and gold-tipped wings spread in flight. Jeweled eyes gazed skyward from a purple hood. Yellow and orange and red flames licked at its talons. A long, graceful tail curved out of sight down her back. Drawn by its haunting beauty, Tyler felt compelled to touch it, lightly brushing his fingers across it.

He heard Beth's sharp intake of breath, and felt the tremble ripple through her under his fingertips. Her pulse fluttered rapidly at the spot where her red-amber hair brushed the junction of her neck and he thought about kissing her, pressing his lips to her bare shoulder, wrapping his arms around her small waist and pulling her delectable, soft curves against him.

He looked up and his gaze collided with hers in the mirror. Her eyes widened. *She knows what I'm thinking. And it scares her*. He remembered the phone calls she hadn't acknowledged and slowly lowered his hand.

"It's beautiful," he said. *You're beautiful.* "What kind of bird is it?"

"A phoenix."

Beth drew in a slow, deep breath to settle her jangled nerves. She'd been certain he was going to kiss her, was disquieted by how much she'd wanted him to, and the intensity of her disappointment that he hadn't. She exchanged her lab coat for a short denim jacket that matched her skirt.

"From Greek mythology?" he asked.

"The word 'phoenix' is Greek, but the myth is more Egyptian."

"It suits you. Have you had it long?"

"Four years." She brushed by him to get her purse from the bottom drawer of the file cabinet.

When she looked up a moment later, Tyler had tipped his cap back on his head, and with his hands thrust in the pockets of his trousers, was studying one of the enlarged photographs on the wall behind the cabinet—a young woman, naked from the waist up, her back turned discreetly to the camera to show the elaborately tattooed vine of wild red roses that followed the curve of her body from hip to shoulder. It was one Beth had been particularly proud of. She'd used different line weights, or no line at all, varying the shades to make skin and design appear as one. The colors were bold, yet gave the illusion of being delicate. It had taken her three months to complete. She foolishly found herself hoping Tyler would like it. Foolish because she knew she didn't need his approval.

"Did you do this?" he asked.

"Yes."

"I'm impressed."

His straightforward honesty brought a smile to her lips. "Thank you."

For the moment at least, the tension between them seemed to have eased. He turned to lean his hips against the cabinet and crossed one foot over the other, striking a casual pose that could have come from the pages of a fashion magazine, yet Beth didn't think he was even aware of it. She supposed that was part of his appeal. There was an unconscious grace in the way he wore his tailored uniform, from the perfect knot in his black bowtie, to the shine of his leather oxfords. Her gaze skimmed up his long, muscled legs and broad shoulders, to the cap tipped back on his raven black hair.

"What is it?" he asked, watching her.

She gave a breathless laugh. "I was just

wondering what kind of tattoo would look good on you."

One dark eyebrow lifted high on his forehead and his smile took an amused slant. "What have you come up with?"

"I haven't decided." Then slinging the long strap of her purse over her shoulder, she explained, "A tattoo has to reflect something of its wearer."

"And you don't know me well enough, yet."

The implication in his low, husky voice sent nervous anticipation skittering through Beth. She would get to know him better, that voice promised. Would already know him better, his gray eyes accused, if she had returned his calls.

"Why did you choose a phoenix?" he asked.

Anticipation became a sobering chill up Beth's spine. "I was celebrating my divorce."

"I'm sorry."

She tipped her head and regarded him with a small frown. "Why would you be sorry?"

"Ending a marriage can't be easy. Some people might mark their calendar to remember the date, but you chose something much more permanent." He'd closed the short distance between them as he spoke. Reaching out, he lightly caressed her cheek. Once. Just enough for the breath to catch in her throat.

"It must have been very hard on you," he said softly. "Maybe hard enough that you wanted a constant reminder to never make that mistake again?"

Beth willed herself to remain still. She didn't want him to know how painfully close he'd come to the truth. "Did you major in psychology, Mr. Stone?"

"Actually, I dropped out of high school, Ms. Heart."

Beth acknowledged this bit of information with a blink.

"And you're changing the subject," he told her.

"I'd rather not discuss my marriage." She started for the door.

"Sooner or later we are going to have to talk about it."

Beth whirled round to glare at him. "Why can't you just leave it alone?"

"Because I think it has an effect on what's happening between us."

Fear jagged through her. She swallowed hard to keep it from choking her. "What is happening between us?"

His gray eyes darkened. "You tell me. Why didn't you return my messages? And don't bother telling me you were too busy. I'm a little smarter than that."

Beth brought her chin up. "You're angry."

"You're damn right I am."

But there was some other emotion eating at him, too, she realized. Uncertainty? Vulnerability? It found its way through her defenses and tugged at her conscience.

"You say you want to see me again, but you don't return my calls. Is this some kind of game to you?"

"No," she insisted quickly. Memories of the endless mind games Eric had played on her, for the sole purpose of manipulating her, pushed their way to the foreground of her thoughts. Her stomach took a sickening lurch.

She moistened her suddenly dry lips and met Tyler's look. "I don't want there to be any games between us."

"Then what do you want, Beth? I need to know."

"I want..." Too much. Looking at him, seeing the desire to understand in his expression, made her fears seem foolish and unbiased. She didn't want to hurt him, that much she did know. She was tempted to believe he was all he seemed, that he was a man who would love her without pushing her into a corner, a man who wouldn't try to change her or control her.

But even if that were true, was she prepared to let a man, any man, into her life again? Was she willing to risk her hard-earned independence?

"I don't know, Tyler," she admitted, trying to be as honest with him as she could over something she didn't have the answer to.

"Can you at least tell me if I'm wasting my time by being here?" he asked, his frustration evident in the deep rasp of his voice.

Tension filled the silence between them. Tyler couldn't read the emotions that played across Beth's heart-shaped face. She stared at him, yet seemed almost not to be seeing him at all, but rather some distant memory that haunted her. He held his breath, waiting, feeling his chances slipping away. His lungs ached for air, but he ignored them. He'd walked out on a limb coming here tonight. He didn't know if she was going to take his hand and guide him back, or push him off.

"No," she finally said, her voice a whisper, "you're not."

Tyler sucked in a deep breath, drawing the fragrance of wild roses, her fragrance, into his lungs. He held it for a long moment before slowly letting it, letting her, go. She watched him, her fine, pale brows drawn together in uncertainty. She wasn't entirely comfortable with her decision, he knew. Her vulnerability stirred an ache in him to hold her. He longed to quiet the fear that held her captive. But he also knew if he touched her now he may not be able to control his longing. The line between comfort and seduction was a very thin one.

Again, he made himself take an emotional step back. He gave her a crooked smile. "Then how about that tour?"

Her mouth curved. "All right."

It was quickly apparent that Beth loved her work. Her face was animated as she moved to the counter and deposited her purse. "All of this—" she indicated the photos on the walls with a sweep of her arm, "—is the artsy stuff I have fun with. But there's another side to tattooing that most people aren't aware of."

Tyler took his garrison cap off and laid it next to her purse. "The medical side that you talked about before," he said, combing his fingers briefly through his hair.

"Yes." She pulled a fat, three-ring binder from under the counter. "You asked me how I met Sam." She plopped the binder down and began flipping through the plastic sleeved pages as she spoke. "It was about two years ago." She found what she was looking for and slid the binder in front of him. "She'd been in an car accident. Her surgeon did a marvelous job, but he couldn't avoid some of the scarring, as you can see."

Tyler stared at the face in the first photograph, the white line that ran from brow to cheek and another along the hairline. He couldn't believe this was the same young woman who'd winked and flirted with him just days ago. The second photo was the Sam he knew, the scars no longer visible.

"And you did this with tattooing?"

"That's just the beginning."

She showed him photos of burn victims—a woman whose mouth had been reconstructed from scar tissue, her left eyebrow all but gone. In the accompanying photo, her features had been restored. There was a black man with white splotches on his face and neck, a condition Beth called Vitiligo. By carefully mixing pigments, she'd blended the discolored areas with the man's natural skin tone. The scars of a dog bite on a young woman's face, gone. Mastectomy scars all but erased. Photo after photo of people with imperfections that had been artfully disguised.

"This is amazing," Tyler said.

Beth smiled. "I've been fortunate to have

found an art form I love and helps people feel good about themselves at the same time."

"You call it art. Something like this must be expensive."

"It depends on the patient. If somebody can't afford my normal rate, I give him or her a discount. And I've done some work for free. No one should have to go through life permanently scarred."

She said the last part so quietly that Tyler looked at her. He doubted she was aware of how exposed her own scars were at that moment.

And in that instant, Tyler realized how easy it would be to love her. As cool and unapproachable as she would have him believe, she'd shown him the warm, compassionate heart that beat within her. She was an artist and a healer, and he was falling for her hard.

"Why are you looking at me that way?" she whispered.

"What way is that?"

He heard the dry click in her throat when she tried to swallow. "Like you can see through me."

"Not through," he murmured, "into."

"Don't."

She started to move away, but he captured her arm and pulled her to him. "Why does that scare you?" He wove his fingers through the hair at the back of her head and gently held her so she couldn't look away. "What are you afraid I'll see?"

"Nothing. I just..."

He touched his mouth to the corner of hers. "What, Beth?" He dragged his lips to the opposite corner. He couldn't help himself. She was too tempting to resist. "You just what?"

"I just..." her breath caught, "...want you to kiss me," she said on a warm exhale.

It wasn't the answer he'd been looking for, but there was no way he was going to deny her. Not when it was what he'd wanted to do from the moment he'd walked through the door.

Heat exploded between them as he shaped his mouth to hers, his hands gliding to her back, pressing her breasts, her belly, her hips against him. Her arms came around his waist and she clung to him, her small hands bunching the back of his jacket. Her lips parted on a sigh and he took advantage, his tongue exploring, teasing. Like a sweet, potent wine, the taste of her fogged his head and flooded his senses. He ached to feel her caress on his naked flesh.

As if sharing his need, she thrust her hands up between them and pulled the knot of his tie loose. Her fingers were warm against his throat as she worked at the top button of his shirt.

"Elizabeth?"

"Hmm?" She gave a small smile of satisfaction when the button freed, and immediately started on the next.

"Didn't your mother ever tell you not to play with matches?"

"Mmm," she pushed the collar of his shirt open and pressed her lips to the base of his throat, just above his T-shirt. "I could start a fire," she murmured. Her breath cooled the spot she'd just kissed. Then incredibly, she bit him, lightly, her teeth scraping his sensitized skin.

Tyler gave an agonized groan. "Lady, you've already done that." He cupped her bottom and pulled her against him, hard. When she looked up at him, her mouth formed a startled O and he crushed his lips to it.

If Beth had thought herself in control, he quickly proved her wrong. Her head reeled with the force of his kiss. Her heart jackhammered in her chest. She clutched the open collar of his shirt and held on. She'd told him no games, and no games it was. The man was real. The feelings he ignited in her were real. He'd not only conquered fire, he *was* fire.

When he pulled back, the only thing she could think of to say was an idiotic *wow*, so she said nothing.

"You look surprised," he murmured.

Stunned is more like it. Beth frowned at the small indentations on his neck. Her teeth marks, she realized, and felt the color rise in her cheeks. She disentangled her fingers from his shirt and clumsily smoothed it closed.

"I don't know how that happened," she muttered.

"It's not hard to understand." She looked up and he gave her one of those lopsided smiles that did funny things to her balance. "You're a beautiful, compassionate woman and you've got me wanting you so much I can't sleep at night."

"Oh."

His deep laugh tumbled over her. "That sums it up pretty good." He kissed the end of her nose and released her. "I'm going to go," he said, retrieving his garrison cap and positioning it on his head, "while I still can."

Thankful for the reprieve, Beth grabbed her

purse. "I'll walk out with you."

He helped her with her trenchcoat, then followed her out of the studio and waited while she locked up.

"Can I give you a ride?" he asked.

"No." She turned and bumped into him. The desire was still there. The heat. The temptation to drag him back inside and finish what they'd started. "Thank you," she said with a self-conscious laugh, her gaze skittering from his, "but I really could use the air."

"All right," he said on a soft chuckle that told her he identified with her need. They crossed the thick navy and mauve carpet to the elevator and Tyler punched the 'down' button. "Have dinner with me Wednesday then."

"Why Wednesday?"

"It's the only night next week Dan can work."

"Dan?"

"Daniel O'Connor, my relief driver."

"I see." The elevator doors whooshed open and they stepped inside the brightly lit cubicle. "Did you have somewhere in mind?" she asked as the doors slid shut.

"My place."

Beth's pulse tripped over itself.

"I make a mean pizza soufflé," he said.

She gave a bemused smile. "What is a pizza soufflé?"

"Come to my house Wednesday, around seven, and I'll show you."

"You really think you have me figured out, don't you?"

He laughed. "What makes you say that?"

"You know I can't cook, so you tempt me with food."

"Is it working?" His eyes glinted wickedly.

"It's going to take more than catering to my stomach to win me over, Tyler Stone." Her mouth quirked. "But it's a good place to start. Wednesday at seven would be fine."

"Good." He pulled a business card and pen from his lapel pocket. "Here's my address," he said, writing on the back of the card. When he was done, he tucked the pen away and held the card out to her. "I know Holly is looking forward to meeting you."

The card slipped through Beth's fingers. "Oh—sorry."

"I'll get it."

Beth drew in a quiet, steadying breath as Tyler stooped to retrieve the card. She couldn't help feeling like she'd just been asked to meet his parents for the first time. She imagined the curious stares. The embarrassing questions.

What do you say to a teenager whose father you've just sunk your teeth into in the heat of passion?

"Here you go."

Beth blinked. "Thank you." She took the card from him and tucked it in a pocket of her purse. "Are you sure this is all right with your daughter?" she asked, then at his questioning look, rushed on, "I mean, the two of you must not have a lot of time to spend together, with your busy schedule and her going to school. I wouldn't want to intrude."

"You won't be intruding, Beth." Hooking a finger under her chin, he lifted her face and brushed his lips lightly across hers.

Beth was vaguely aware of the elevator doors opening, then closing again. He was so good at that, she thought, making her forget where she was, who she was. And he knew it, too, dammit. She felt his smile against her lips before he lowered his hand and turned to push the 'open' button.

The elevator doors parted. He followed her through the foyer and out the main entrance of the medical plaza. The chilly December evening was clear, the air crisp. There would be frost in the morning. Beth lifted her collar higher.

"You're sure I can't give you that ride?"

Tyler asked her again.

She eyed the long white limousine at the curb, then the man at her side. He hadn't bothered to re-button his shirt and his tie hung loose around his neck. He looked...delicious. There was more than one kind of hunger he could cater to, she thought, her pulse taking another uneven bump.

And right now she was just hungry enough that getting into his fancy car would be a mistake. "I'm sure. Good night, Tyler."

He tipped his cap to her. "Good night, pretty lady."

7

Tyler grasped the basketball with both hands and tucked it close to his belly. The frigid night air against his gray sweats, damp with perspiration, cooled his heated skin. He extended his elbows and inclined his torso forward to protect the ball. Holly, the defense, was behind him. He thrust his head and shoulders toward the free-throw line—an imaginary area on the carport's concrete pad— as if intending to pivot in that direction.

He knew the instant his daughter was caught off guard. He drop-stepped, executed a two-hand power dribble and shot the lay-up. The ball dropped through the basket without touching the hoop.

He thrust his arms into a wide V above his

head. "Two points!" he declared with a suppressed shout. He didn't want Mrs. Huntington from next door coming down on him for disturbing her evening TV program.

"It's not over yet!" Holly rushed in, the haphazard ponytail she'd pulled her dark hair into whipping behind her, and caught the rebound. She dribbled the ball away from the basket, out of Tyler's reach.

He crouched, arms and legs spread, ready for her attack. "Show me what you've got," he said and flashed her a broad grin.

Holly's answering smile had a sly tip to it. She continued to dribble the ball, her eyes never leaving his. "You won't know what hit you."

She was right. Her gaze flicked to the left and she made a short, jabbing step in that direction. Tyler moved to intercept and realized too late he'd been faked out. Holly's purple sweats were a blurred shadow as she charged to her right. Tyler turned in time to see her stutter-step, bring both feet together and jump. The ball rolled off her fingertips and into the basket.

She caught the rebound and dribbled away from him. "Give?" she asked, laughing.

"Not a chance." He moved toward her and

she neatly back-stepped, pivoting out of his reach.

Damn, she's good, Tyler thought with a mixture of pride and regret. If only she'd taken more of an interest in the sport. She could have easily been recruited by any number of college coaches. But like a lot of other things, she'd tried it for a year and lost interest.

"A flibbertigibbet," Grandma Lou had been fond of calling her. "That child's got the where-with-all to do anything she sets her mind to. It'll be interesting to see what she does with it."

Tyler was beginning to wonder if his daughter would ever "set her mind" to something. How he wished Grandma Lou was here now. He could use some of her straight-forward, down-to-earth advice. And not just about Holly's indifference toward college.

"How'd the party go?" he asked.

"Okay."

"Did Tony notice your new dress?"

Instead of answering, Holly tried for a basket and missed. Muttering something Tyler chose not to hear, she caught the rebound and moved away from the hoop, the ball resounding against the concrete.

"I'm sorry, baby."

"It doesn't matter."

"Yeah, it does." Tyler moved into position, as if making ready to grab for the ball, but his attention was on his daughter and the frown that worried her forehead. "Want to talk about it?"

She glanced up at him, then away, the contact brief. But Tyler saw the hurt in her dark eyes. He silently cursed the boy responsible for putting it there.

Holly pivoted and charged for the basket again. With the grace of a pro, she leaped and sunk the ball in a two-handed jam. Landing under the hoop, she turned and looked at him, ignoring the ball as it bounced away from her. "I'm four inches taller than the guy." She threw her hands up in disgust. "What's to talk about?"

Tyler grabbed the ball, shot and missed. "Damn," he muttered, but the oath had nothing to do with basketball. He'd forgotten that what he considered an asset, his daughter regarded as a physical flaw. For a moment, he'd forgotten about the fragile nature of the teenage ego.

Holly took the ball and moved to center court. Tyler crouched and braced his hands on his knees. "So," he said as matter-of-factly as possible, "you thought you liked him and he turned out to be a jerk. He's the loser, not you."

"I didn't like him!" Holly blurted. The sharp whack of the ball on the carport pad emphasized her words. Tyler held his breath, expecting Mrs. Huntington's booming voice any second.

One, two, three more times Holly drove the ball against the concrete before she caught it and hugged it to her. "I mean, not really," she said, her voice lower but no less frustrated. She turned and Tyler's heart tightened at the turmoil in her expression. "But I wanted him to like me, you know?" She gave a harsh little laugh. "Is that dumb, or what?"

"No, baby, it's not." Tyler went to her. "There's nothing dumb about wanting to be accepted." He pushed some loose strands of hair from her face. "But you need to accept yourself first. You're a beautiful young woman, Holly. Don't let anybody tell you otherwise."

"You're my dad. You're supposed to say that." She gave a reluctant smile. "But thanks anyway, for calling me a woman."

Tyler suddenly felt a hundred years old. "There'll be other guys," he told her, the sharp pang to his heart adding another couple of years. *And if any of them harm a hair on your head, I'll kill them personally.* "Taller ones," he added with a wry smile.

She gave him a quick kiss on the cheek. "Thanks, Dad. I love you."

"I love you, too, baby."

"So," she stepped away and began dribbling the ball again, "are you going to tell me what you're doing out here?"

"What do you mean?" he asked. But it was a redundant question. His daughter knew him too well.

"I mean, it's like freezing out here and you're shooting hoops. So, something must be bothering you."

Tyler drew in a deep breath. It was now or never. "I've invited somebody—a woman—to have dinner with us next Wednesday."

Holly caught the basketball, tucked it under her arm, and stared at him. "A woman? As in a date?"

Tyler felt their roles shift briefly. "I suppose you could call it that," he replied, although *date* seemed wrong somehow. Too innocent.

"Who is she?"

"Her name's Elizabeth Heart."

"Isn't she the one who gave that man a bloody nose in the limo?"

"Yeah."

"I didn't know you were dating her."

"I haven't been, exactly. We sort of bumped into each other." *And ignited*. The memory of it still burned in him. "I did a couple of small repairs for her—"

"That ugly Santa was hers, wasn't it?"

"That's right."

"Why didn't you tell me?"

Because it happened so fast. Like watching an action movie, he'd been swept in with the first scene and taken on a breathless ride. And he hadn't been sure how long the ride would last. Because he hadn't expected the feelings that overwhelmed him. And because he'd wanted to keep Beth to himself, at least for a little while. He only hoped that if she found out he'd lied to her about Holly's eagerness to meet her, she would understand.

"I didn't want you making a big deal out of it," he said.

"You've never done this before." The guarded accusation in his daughter's voice told him it *was* a big deal.

"I never wanted to before," he answered truthfully. He'd never found a woman he could care enough for to want to bring her into his home, until now. He'd devoted himself to being a father, had made the conscious choice to keep his private life and social life separate.

But Beth had changed all of that.

Holly began to dribble the ball again, her back to him.

"Talk to be, baby," Tyler coaxed.

"I'm not stupid, Dad." She continued to bounce the ball, continued to avoid looking at him. "I know if it wasn't for me, there would have been more women in your life."

Tyler reached in and grabbed the ball. Holly shot him a startled look. "Don't ever think I regret my decision to be a father to you," he told her, his tone more stern than he intended.

Tears pooled in Holly's eyes. Tyler tucked the basketball under one arm and put the other around her shoulders, pulling her to him. "I did it because I wanted to," he said with gentle insistence, "not because I had to. I thought you knew that."

She gave a quick shrug, as if it wasn't important. But Tyler knew it was or they wouldn't be out here playing basketball with frost biting at their extremities.

"I guess I just needed to, you know, hear you say it."

Her voice had become small, and for a moment, she was his little girl again. He saw a tear roll down her cheek, but she hurriedly swiped it away. Tyler hugged her and kissed her cooled temple.

"I'll remember to remind you of it more often."

"This is so weird," she said on a choked laugh.

"What's that, baby?"

She sniffed and laid her head on his shoulder. "I never thought of you as somebody's boyfriend before."

Boyfriend. Another too-tame word.

Antagonist, without a doubt. Lover, he could only hope. Beth's hot and cold attitude had kept him guessing just where he fit in.

She'd begun to trust him tonight, but he doubted she was aware of it. If he'd learned anything about her at all, it was that she didn't trust easily. And the phoenix proved how deeply she could be affected when that trust was abused. He wanted her trust. He wanted to be the one she opened her heart to. He'd glimpsed her passion, had tasted it on her lips. Hell, he'd even felt its bite. His body stirred at the memory of her teeth grazing his skin.

He wanted to be the one to free her of the fears that had her denying that passion. It scared him to think how strongly he wanted.

And he wasn't a man who scared easy.

"It feels kinda weird to me, too," he

admitted, then turned and together he and his daughter made their way toward the house.

~~~

There, astride the massive white horse, his gray eyes searching through the flames for her. Her hero. She reached out to him. The flames licked at her hand but she didn't pull back, despite the pain. The certainty he would save her from the blond man standing just outside the ring of fire was that strong.

The man in black saw her. Awareness flared in his taut, handsome face. He dug his heels into the steed's heaving sides and man and horse charged toward her. His large, strong hand enveloped hers and swept her up behind him. She circled his lean waist and buried her face in his broad back. His heart beat hard and heavy beneath her cheek. His fragrance, wild and untamed, filled her nostrils like a drug. His heat coiled through her until she felt boneless. She felt herself falling, her arms no longer strong enough to hold on.

"I will catch you," he told her, his deep voice a caress that flowed over her skin. He held her and together they fell, their bodies joined, becoming one as they plunged through space...

Beth jerked awake. Her gaze darted through the darkness, seeking the familiar, half expecting to find the earth falling away below her and stars so close she could touch them. She wrapped her arms around herself, believing she could still feel him, aching to hold onto the sensation.

Too soon the dream fog lifted and she was in her room, in her bed, alone.

She pulled the covers to her chin and lay staring at the ceiling. The dreams had become more intense. More erotic. The man in black was no longer just her rescuer. He'd become her lover.

A tremor shook her body.

She didn't need a hero, someone to rescue her from evil. Because there was no evil, she insisted.

But a lover?

Yes. He had her wanting that. He had her aching for much more than a touch, a kiss. But Tyler Stone wasn't the kind of man to settle for a simple, short-term romance.

And he wasn't a patient man. He saw too much. Knew too much too soon. She'd only agreed to dinner, but she had the unshakable feeling she'd accepted an invitation to heartache.

8

Tyler lived in southeast Portland, near Mount Tabor. The square, two-story house with white clapboard siding, dormer windows and a wide porch, was easy to find. At two minutes to seven, Beth squeezed her little car between Tyler's Jeep and a mid-sized pickup at the curb and turned off the engine. She'd spent the past forty-eight hours thinking of ways to get out of tonight's dinner. Unfortunately, none of the excuses she came up with could hide the real reason she hadn't wanted to come. She was scared silly.

"What can happen with his seventeen-year-old daughter in the same room?" Sam had asked, completely unsympathetic to Beth's reservations.

Beth had to admit, her friend had a point. But that didn't make her any more comfortable about being here. What would Holly think of her? Would she resent having another woman in her home? Would she think her dinner guest's tapered beige slacks and over-sized dusty violet cardigan frumpy?

Beth gave a self-deprecating growl and jammed her keys in her purse. It wasn't like her to be so concerned over what kind of impression she made.

But then it wasn't like her to go to a man's house for dinner, either.

The limousine took up the entire carport, its front bumper extending out beneath a basketball hoop and tattered net mounted to the eaves. As Beth got out of her car, a tall, lean figure in black, his garrison cap pulled low, rushed from the house, skirted the front of the limousine and yanked open the right rear door.

Tyler, Beth thought. And he appeared to be in a hurry.

Frowning, she thrust her hands in the deep pockets of her trenchcoat. It didn't matter that this could be the excuse she'd been looking for to get out of dinner. For him to take off without so much as an explanation went beyond rude.

He was leaning inside the back of the car

when she marched up behind him and asked, "Going somewhere?"

His head thwacked against the top of the door frame. A colorful oath followed close on its heels. Something about the voice wasn't right. But before Beth had time to realize why, his garrison cap landed at her feet and she found herself staring at a startling shock of curly copper hair. When the man straightened, he was at least two inches taller than Tyler.

"Ohmygosh," Beth muttered. "Are you hurt?"

He appeared to be in his late twenties, maybe early thirties, his attractive face tanned and outdoorsy. He gingerly felt the back of his head.

"No, ma'am. Lucky for me I hit the hardest part of my body." He chuckled at his own joke and continued, "But you really shouldn't sneak up on people that way."

"I'm sorry. This is so embarrassing. I thought you, well, that you were—"

"Tyler," he finished, his generous mouth pulling into a knowing smile. "You must be Elizabeth."

"Yes. And you're either Daniel, or a very-well dressed car thief."

"Daniel O'Connor." He thrust the hand that

wasn't massaging the back of his head out to her. "It's a pleasure to meet you, ma'am."

"I doubt that." Beth took his hand and was surprised at how big and warm it was. Like shaking paws with a teddy bear. "Please, call me Beth. Ma'am makes me feel like I'm somebody's grandmother."

Daniel's eyes glinted in the light from the porch. They were periwinkle blue.

"Nobody's about to make that mistake, Beth. I see now why Ty hasn't talked about anything but you lately."

Beth felt the tips of her ears warm. "What exactly has he been saying about me?"

"Sorry," Daniel gave a deep, jovial laugh, "but Ty's not just my employer, he's my friend. I'd like to keep it that way."

"Your loyalty is noble."

"It's called self-preservation." He retrieved his cap and dusted it off with a swipe of his big hand. "I'd better get out of here, or there are going to be some disappointed folks at the Benson Hotel." He put his cap on and cringed.

"I am sorry about your head," Beth said again. "Maybe you should put some ice on it?"

"I'll be fine. But thanks for your concern." He regarded her a moment, his blue eyes direct. "Did you really think Ty would try to sneak out on you tonight?"

Beth had to admit the idea sounded pretty silly—now. She sighed. "It crossed my mind."

"It's none of my business," Daniel stepped aside to close the car door, then leaned with a hand braced against the edge of the limo's roof, "but there's something you should know about Tyler Stone."

Beth wasn't sure she wanted to hear what this big man had to tell her.

"Ty and I met when we took some GED classes together, almost twelve years ago. I guess next to that little girl of his, I'm about as close to the man as anybody. We've had us some good times together, but I've never seen him so tangled up inside over a woman before. He called me five times if he called me at all to make sure I could take this job tonight. This dinner is that important to him."

Beth stood speechless.

"Well, I can see I've said enough." Daniel winked and touched the brim of his cap to her. "Enjoy your evening, Beth."

She stepped out of the way and watched as he pulled the long car into the street and drove off. She shivered, suddenly aware of the cold. *No*, she thought, hunching her shoulders and casting a furtive glance at her own car, *I shouldn't be here. Tyler is taking this much too seriously.*

"Hello, Elizabeth."

She gave a startled scream. "Dammit, Tyler!" She whirled and collided with his chest. He took her arm to steady her. Her brain briefly registered blue jeans and a hunter-green shirt with the sleeves rolled to the elbows, before meeting his gray eyes, ardent and unsettlingly familiar. She'd missed them, missed *him*, she realized, and resisted cursing him a second time.

"Don't sneak up on me like that!"

"Sorry." But his easy dimpled smile said otherwise. He tugged gently and her body made contact with his thighs, hips, stomach. "You're trembling again."

"Because you scared the wits out of me." But that was a lie. The momentary fright he'd given her had nothing to do with her body's disarming reaction to his.

Tyler had been sure she would call at the last minute and cancel. He needed the contact to convince himself she was really there. He lifted his free hand to her flushed cheek.

"I see you've met Dan." Her face warmed under his fingers and Tyler chuckled softly. "He seems to have that affect on women."

The sudden flare of awareness in her cat-green eyes as she stared up at him fanned a fire in his groin. Her red-amber hair wreathed her face in wild curls. The urge to bury himself in it, in her, was strong. If not for his daughter upstairs, he could have easily made love to this woman right there in full light of the porch. It would certainly give Mrs. Huntington something to gossip about for awhile.

"Aw, hell," he muttered and settled for a kiss. Her lips warmed quickly to his, parting without hesitation. He pushed his fingers through her hair as he tasted her sweetness, felt her hunger in the way she kissed him back.

When it was over, the color in her cheeks had deepened as though her response to him embarrassed her. Tyler found it endearing. His fingers untangled from her hair to caress the delicate line of her jaw.

"You look beautiful tonight."

"Thank you." She sighed and said softly, "So do you."

He smiled and tenderly kissed the end of her nose. He knew how hard it must have been for her to admit and he was flattered. "Thank you." Reluctantly, he pulled back, maintaining a light hold on her arm. "We'd better go inside before Mrs. Huntington brings out her binoculars."

"You have a nosy neighbor?" Beth let him guide her toward the house.

"Edith Huntington is the eyes and ears of the block. A good woman at heart, but nothing gets by her."

Beth laughed lightly as she preceded Tyler through the front door and into his home. A delicious, pungent aroma, reminiscent of her favorite Italian restaurant on the west side of town, greeted her as she stood in the small entry. To her immediate right, a carpeted stairway and heavy dark wood banister curved to the second floor. A family room opened on her left, its high ceiling latticed in the same dark wood as the banister, the walls painted a soft parchment white. The chocolate-brown couch and recliner had a comfortable, lived-in look, and a profusion of books, framed photos, seashells and colorful candles gave the room a welcomed hominess.

But it was the blaze burning in the brick fireplace directly across from her that captured her attention and drew her in, conjured images of another fire, and a man on a powerful white horse searching for her through the flames...

"May I take your coat?"

She jumped at the sound of Tyler's voice

directly behind her. "Oh—yes." She felt the heat creep into her face again. Annoyance made her clumsy and she fumbled with the buttons of her trenchcoat.

Tyler cupped her shoulders and drew her back against his chest. She leaned into him just a little—just enough to let his solid strength steady her.

"Would it help if I told you I'm as nervous as you are?" he confessed, his deep voice a warm whisper in her ear.

That wasn't possible. She was the one out of her element. She was the one having the disturbing, sensual dreams. "Don't tell me you lied about being able to cook."

"You're forgetting the breakfast I made at your place," he scolded.

Forget how at home he'd looked in her kitchen? Or that it had been the first time a man had ever cooked for her? Not for awhile.

"Anybody can scramble eggs," she said. Although that wasn't entirely true. Hers always managed to come out rubbery.

Tyler chuckled and helped her remove her coat. "Don't worry," he said, turning to the coat tree behind him, "Grandma Lou taught me a thing or two in the kitchen."

The sound of someone rushing down the

stairs drew Beth's attention in that direction. A strikingly attractive young woman in slim white jeans and baggy flannel shirt rounded the corner and stopped short on the landing. Wide, dark eyes regarded Beth a moment before she descended the bottom flight of steps. Despite the difference in eye and hair color, there was no denying the resemblance to Tyler. She was only a couple of inches shorter than her father and towered over Beth's five foot five by half a head. Beth found it a bit intimidating.

"Holly, I'd like you to meet Elizabeth Heart."

Holly's gaze darted from Beth to her father, then back. Beth got the distinct impression the young woman did indeed resent her being there. She was afforded a polite, but brief, smile. "Hello, Miss Heart."

Beth cringed at the formal greeting. "It's a pleasure to meet you, Holly."

Tyler's daughter regarded her a second longer, then went to the coat tree and grabbed a huge black wool jacket.

"Where are you going?" Tyler asked, clearly surprised.

Holly gave him a quick glance from the corner of her eye and pushed her arms into the sleeves of her coat. "To Karen's, remember?"

"No I don't."

"I told you this afternoon." She put a floppy-brimmed knit hat on and made for the door. "Mrs. Roberst popped a test on us for tomorrow and Karen and I are going to study together."

Beth knew Holly was lying by the way she never quite made eye-contact with her father. If there was one thing she didn't want to do, it was get caught in the middle of a father-daughter argument. Especially when she suspected she was the cause. Nor did she like the sudden prospect of being left alone with Tyler in his domain.

"You haven't eaten," Tyler stated, his voice tight.

"That's okay." Holly flung the door open. "Karen's mom said I could have dinner with them." She paused and glanced at Beth. "It was nice to meet you." Her gaze just missed her father. "Bye, Dad."

Tyler watched in stunned silence as his daughter rushed from the house.

"Maybe I should go, too," Beth offered.

Tyler shifted his attention to the woman beside him. She looked fragile and wonderful, and in spite of what had just transpired, he didn't regret her being there. "I don't know what that was all about," he said, "but I'd like you to stay."

"It's obvious I make your daughter uncomfortable."

"That's my fault, not yours."

"And how did you arrive at that conclusion?"

"This is the first time I've ever invited a woman into our home," he admitted.

She doesn't believe me. He saw it in the way she regarded him, warily, a small frown furrowing her brow.

"I guess you were right when you said we have more in common than a fondness for cookies," she finally said.

"What do you mean?"

"You're not in the habit of inviting—" she hesitated, moistening her lips, "—and I'm not in the habit of accepting."

"Why did you, Beth?"

"To find out what pizza soufflé is, of course."

Tyler's laughter echoed through the big old house. "It's ready when you are. Unless you'd rather have a glass of wine first?"

It was an innocent enough question, Beth decided, but a picture of herself snuggled next to Tyler on that comfortable couch, sipping wine on an empty stomach and attempting casual conversation, prompted her to reply firmly, "I'd prefer to eat now."

"I was hoping you'd say that." He smiled, and in a move that was so casual it surprised her, he took her hand and led her through the family room and a pair of sliding glass doors to a formal dining area.

A maple oval table, set with white linen and surrounded by six spindle-backed chairs, dominated the center of the room. Here the walls were papered in a soft mint stripe pattern and a built-in hutch took up most of one end. Beth was drawn to the glass figurines, many of them animals, and the bone china with a delicate iris pattern that crowded the glassed-in shelves.

"Grandma liked to collect pretty things," Tyler said as he gathered up one of the place settings at the table. "They're a pain to dust, but I don't have the heart to put them away."

His sentiment touched her. She thought of her own grandmother's pretty things and endured the familiar stab of bitter remorse that accompanied it. "No," she agreed, "they belong out where you can see them."

Tyler pulled a chair away from one of the remaining place settings at the end of the table.

"Make yourself comfortable. I'll get the food."

"Is there anything I can help with?"

He tossed her a book of matches. "Light the candles?"

"I think I can manage that."

He gave her a warm smile. "I'll only be a minute."

He disappeared through a swinging door to the right. Beth caught a glimpse of turquoise tile and cream-colored cabinets before the door swung closed. She'd barely struck the first match when Tyler reappeared carrying a steaming casserole dish between his oven-mitted hands. He set it on a cast iron turret, then hurried from the room again. By the time Beth had the tapers lit, he'd produced an enormous tossed salad and a bottle of red wine.

"Everything looks great," she said, taking a seat.

He stood next to her and poured the wine, his dark lashes shadowing his eyes, the long-stemmed goblets fragile looking in his strong, capable hands. Her gaze was level with his lean waist where his shirt tucked into his jeans. She curled her fingers in her lap, disturbed by the strong urge to touch him. Her eyes lifted to the open collar of his shirt and the hot, vivid memory of how he'd tasted swept through her.

"I hope you brought your appetite." He looked from the goblet in his hand and caught her watching him.

Beth felt the blood rush to her face. She quickly leaned over the casserole dish, hoping to blame her sudden color on the steam rising from the lightly browned, puffy crust. "This smells wonderful," she said, inhaling deeply. "What's in it?"

"Milk-soaked bread, seasoned tomato sauce and slices of mozzarella layered together. Then I poured beaten eggs and grated Parmesan over the top."

Beth stared at him, brows arched.

Tyler chuckled and took his seat. "Trust me."

Not on your life. It was much too risky when just looking at him had her fantasizing things that simply couldn't be.

Tyler saw her withdrawal and determined not to let her get away with it this time. He spooned a helping of soufflé onto her plate, then took her fork and held a bite up to her mouth.

"Open."

"This is silly. I can feed myself."

"I'm sure you can," he said, then smiled as she took the offered bite and began chewing.

"But isn't this more fun?"

"It's a good way for you to go hungry." She took the fork from him. "And this," she said, lifting another bite to her mouth, "is delicious."

"I'm glad you like it."

He served the salad—assorted greens, julienne carrots, button mushrooms and thinly sliced radishes. Balsamic vinegar and olive oil melded delectably on Beth's palette. "You said your grandmother taught you how to cook?"

"She got tired of coming home to peanut butter sandwiches and canned soup."

"You stayed home with Holly then, while your grandmother worked?"

"We alternated shifts. I worked nights and watched Holly during the day, while Grandma Lou ran her real estate office."

"When did you sleep?"

A smile hovered on his mouth. "I didn't."

While they ate, Tyler talked about the various jobs he'd had—pumping gas at an all-night service station, throwing together tacos for a 24-hour drive-thru, pushing a broom for a janitorial firm—whatever he could get with his limited education.

"But you went back later and earned your high school equivalency diploma," Beth said, then at his questioning look added, "Your friend, Daniel, told me."

"When Holly was old enough to start school, I enrolled in a general education development course at Portland Community College. Grandma Lou insisted on it."

"She must have been an extraordinary woman."

"She took Holly and me in when nobody else gave a damn."

He said it matter-of-factly, but Beth caught the edge of bitterness in his voice. The edge of some painful memory. She studied the beautiful lines of his face and realized how little she knew about him. What had compelled him to become a father at seventeen? Had it been choice or circumstance? She found herself wondering at the events that had shaped the man, and a feeling of desperation jagged through her. To know the answers was to let him into her life, and probably her heart.

"Still trying to decide what kind of tattoo to give me?" The glint in his pale gray eyes told her he knew full well that wasn't what she was thinking at all.

She shook her head and glanced away. "It's none of my business."

"What do you want to know, Beth? I'll tell you anything."

"Why would you do that?" She looked at him with a small frown. "You barely know me."

He knew her better than she wanted to admit, he thought. For instance, she was curious about him and it frightened her. He knew he'd gained ground by her being here, but he would have to be very careful what he did and said if he wanted this to be more than a one time event.

And she didn't like radishes. She'd discreetly picked them out of her salad and left them on the edge of her plate.

"I'm trying to earn your trust," he said. And before she could voice the negative response he saw in her expression, he lifted the bottle of burgundy and asked, "More wine?"

"Yes." She waited until he'd refilled her glass, then tried again. "Tyler, I—"

"My folks kicked me out when I announced I was leaving school to be a father to my baby."

"I really don't need to hear this."

He told her anyway. He talked about his alcoholic father. Jake Stone had wanted his only son to play football, but Tyler hadn't been interested. And his mother had refused to believe her husband was hitting their child, withdrawing further and further into herself to avoid facing the truth. He told Beth how he'd never seemed to measure up to their expectations, until one day he simply quit trying.

"I became a delinquent, intent on making my dad's life a hell. I figured he was going to beat me either way, so I may as well do something to deserve it."

Beth's heart constricted. Eric had put her on a similar emotional treadmill. No matter how hard she'd tried, she'd never succeeded in making him happy. But she could only imagine how it must have felt when it was your own parents' approval you craved and never got. It occurred to her that a lot of Eric's emotional problems probably stemmed from his relationship with his father. John Wilson had been an over-bearing, demanding man who had often used his sons against each other, Eric's older brother, Harris, being the golden child and Eric the one who never quite measured up. As a result, Eric's sense of inadequacy had caused him to find fault with everyone around him—especially his wife.

"You could have let your relationship with your father destroy you," she said to Tyler. "Instead, it made you strong."

"It made me reckless."

He went on to tell her how he'd met Holly's mother at a party. Her name was Debbie and she'd been fifteen at the time. They'd both been drinking. Before the evening was over, they'd slept together. He wouldn't call it lovemaking because they hadn't been in love. He didn't see her again after that night—until three months later, when she'd told him she was pregnant.

"At first I denied being the father, but Debbie's closest friend swore that Debbie had only had sex that one time, with me. I had no way of proving it. After awhile, I didn't want to. I wanted that baby to be mine."

"Why?" Beth asked.

"Selfishness. It was my chance to have something I could call my own. Someone to love."

He didn't sound selfish at all, Beth thought. He sounded incredibly lonely. How awful it must have been for him, still very much a child himself, to crave love so desperately that he would willingly take responsibility for an illegitimate baby, whether it was his or not, to fill that need.

But Holly was his. The strong family resemblance was proof enough. Had the girl's mother secretly thought herself in love with Tyler? Beth wondered. Or had they simply been young and drunk and irresponsible, as he said?

"Where is Debbie now?"

"I haven't heard from her since that day at the hospital, when she put Holly in my arms and wished me luck."

"She gave you sole custody?"

"Debbie was the oldest of five kids. Her mother was trying to support them alone, on a waitress' pay. They had their reasons for not wanting another mouth to feed."

An all too common story, but tragic never-the-less. "Does Holly know?"

"I've never kept that part of her life a secret. I didn't want her growing up with a bunch of romantic delusions about what happened between her mother and me."

Beth looked at him, really looked at him, as if seeing him for the first time.

"What is it?" he asked, suddenly self-conscious. "Do I have lettuce stuck to my teeth?"

A smile flashed across her features as she shook her head no, then was gone. "You're a complicated man," she told him quietly.

"I'm only trying to be as honest with you as I can, Beth. No secrets."

Tyler saw the sudden closed look in her

expression, felt her resistance like a palpable barrier, and immediately changed the subject.

"There's still some soufflé and salad left," he said, eyeing her empty plate. At some point during their conversation, she'd polished off two helpings of each.

She gave an embarrassed laugh. "Thank you, no. I couldn't eat another bite."

"More wine then? Or coffee?"

"Coffee would be nice."

He smiled. "We can take it in the living room, where it's more comfortable."

"I'll help you clear the table."

"Thanks," Tyler's smile slanted, "but I'm leaving that job for Holly."

He made to stand, but Beth's hand, warm and small on his, stopped him. "Don't be too hard on her, please. I don't want her hating me."

Tyler was gratified that she would care about Holly's feelings after the way Holly had acted. He lifted her hand to his lips. "She won't hate you, Beth." Then twining his fingers with hers, he stood and helped her up from the table. "Go in and make yourself comfortable. I'll get the coffee."

"All right."

He joined her a few minutes later, where she

stood looking at framed photographs on a waist-high bookcase in one corner of the room. Most of the photos were of Holly at various ages, Beth surmised. An adorable child. She wondered if Tyler had looked that cute as a boy. As she took the white china coffee cup from him, she studied the dimples that shaped his mouth and the glint in his slate gray eyes. Yes, she decided with mild regret, he'd been a cute child. And he'd retained just enough of that cuteness to make him dangerous to the female heart now.

"Is this Grandma Lou?" she asked, looking away and pointing to a photo of a stout, dark-haired woman holding an infant in front of a Christmas tree.

"That was taken the day we moved in. Holly was two days old." He laughed. "I was seriously reconsidering my decision to be a father at that point. My new daughter cried all the way from the hospital. But the minute I handed her to her grandma, she quieted down—" he snapped his fingers, "—like that."

"She knew she was home."

"I figured I'd better get a picture of it, in case it didn't last."

His disparaging remark was over-shadowed by the love of a father for his child that Beth saw in his eyes.

"If I'd known about the sleepless nights and endless dirty diapers, I probably would have gotten out of the deal when I had the chance. Do you have any idea how hard it is to get a pair of tights on a two-year-old? Or braid a squirming four-year-old's hair?"

No, she didn't. But she could picture a younger Tyler in that predicament and returned his smile. "I'm surprised you didn't marry out of self-defense."

"When I marry, it'll be because I've found a woman I can't live without." His voice took on a deep timbre that made Beth's skin tingle. His eyes, gone the color of smoke, settled on hers. "I believe in passion, companionship and love that lasts a lifetime."

Her lashes lowered, guarding her eyes. "Good luck," she muttered, and lifted her cup to her lips.

Tyler was determined to know what brought out that reaction in her. He hadn't told her about himself just to hear his own voice. And he sure as hell didn't want or need her sympathy. No, his motives were much more simple than that.

He moved to the couch and sat with his arm draped across the back. "It's your turn," he said, motioning for her to come sit beside him. As her weight settled next to his, the old couch sagged and she was suddenly nestled in the curve of his arm, right where he'd wanted her, her thigh and hip pressed against his. But she wasn't relaxed, by any means. He could feel the tension in her like a guitar wire strung too tight.

"My turn?" she asked vaguely, taking another sip of coffee.

"Talk to me." He set his cup on the table in front of them. "Share something about yourself."

"What do you want to know?"

Anything. Everything. "Tell me about your marriage."

"I don't—"

"— want to discuss it, I remember."

"Then why do you keep bringing it up?"

"Because you do."

"Excuse me?"

She clutched the china cup so tight Tyler half expected it to crumble. He took it from her and set it on the table, next to his.

"Every time you feel I'm getting too close, you use your divorce like a shield."

"That's not true."

"Do I remind you of your ex-husband?"

"No."

She said it without hesitation and he breathed a silent sigh of relief. "Then what is it, Beth? What was so terrible that—" But before he finished the question, he thought he knew the answer. "Did your husband abuse you?" he asked, dread rising like a deadly snake inside him.

Her silence was his answer. Tyler was barely able to rein in the anger that swept through him. *The bastard*. He drew in long, controlled breaths, until the emotion had subsided enough to speak.

"I know what it's like to get the back of a hand from somebody you love," he said gently. "I've been there." He studied the determined set of her jaw and ached to pull her into his arms. But fear prevented him. Suddenly he was afraid to touch her, afraid of setting off some horrible memory for her. He knew about those, too.

"Believe me, Beth, I'd rather die than hurt you." He made a derisive sound deep in his throat. "Hell, I can't even discipline my own daughter when she deserves it."

"It wasn't like that."

"Then explain it to me."

The look in her green eyes was almost

desperate. "It's not something I care to talk about, Tyler. Please accept that."

"Sweet Elizabeth," he murmured, tracing the line of her jaw with his finger. "What's keeping your phoenix heart from flying?"

"What do you mean?"

"A fabled bird that's consumed by fire, then rises from the ashes to begin a new life."

She glanced away. "You've been doing your homework."

"I thought if I knew the story behind the tattoo, I'd know more about the lady wearing it."

"And do you?" she whispered.

"You were in a marriage that consumed you, like the fire consumed the phoenix. Your divorce was your rebirth, the beginning of a new life. But something's keeping you from spreading your wings and setting your heart free."

"You're wrong." She met his gaze with a determined look. "I've spent the last four years living life my way."

"And you think that would change if you and I became lovers?" He absently twined a strand of her hair around his finger.

"We aren't going to make love, Tyler."

"We're already a lot more than friends, and

you know it."

Beth's heart sank at the truth of his words. Still, she held her chin firm and said, "I admit, I care about you. But I won't be pushed into a corner."

"No corners. No strings."

"I don't believe you."

"Then believe this." His lips came down on hers, slowly, his arm tightening around her shoulders ever so slightly, drawing her close, his other hand shaping to her waist.

If he'd pressured her, she could have resisted, but his tenderness was her undoing. She melted against him, her arms coiling around his neck. She discovered she was still hungry as his mouth persisted in its gentle claim. An ache of longing so fierce it took her breath surged through her, arching her into him still more, until he was the only thing that existed.

"We'll do it any way you want," he murmured, and for an instant Beth thought he meant he would make love to her there on the couch, right now, if she said it was what she wanted. And God help her, for a heartbeat it was exactly what she wanted.

"Tyler..."

He kissed her again, effectively driving all

cognitive thought from her brain. When he pulled back the second time, she was breathless.

"I'll do whatever you want," he repeated, his voice low and thick, "but if you think I'm just going to walk away, you're wrong. Understood?"

"Yes." The man had left her no choice. "Damn you," she breathed.

He made a sound deep in his throat that was too harsh to be mistaken for laughter. "If that's what it takes." But his touch was gentle when he brushed the hair back from her face and touched his lips to her forehead. "Did you think you're the only one a relationship between us would affect?"

That was exactly what she'd thought. With Eric, *she* had been the one expected to do all the changing. She'd altered her life to fit his. It stunned her that Tyler had figured it out before she did.

"No, of course not," she whispered.

A slow smile curved his mouth. Beth sighed. She should have known he'd see through her lie.

"Now that we've got that settled," he said, "can I get you some more coffee?"

His smugness irritated. "I have to go." She

pushing out of the deep cushions with some effort.

She could have kicked him for his calm as he stood, that darned sexy smile still dimpling his face and his intent gray eyes quietly watching her. She didn't want to admit she'd expected him to protest, at least a little.

But darn it, she had. And that irritated even more.

"I'll get your coat," he said simply.

9

Tyler was sitting at the kitchen table with his hands wrapped around another cup of coffee when he heard Holly come home. Beth had left an hour earlier.

"Daddy?"

"In here."

His daughter appeared in the open doorway, hands clasped behind her back and a look of innocence in her expression that didn't fool Tyler for a second.

"Is your company gone?" she asked.

"Yes."

Holly worried her lower lip between her teeth a moment, then tucked her dark hair behind her ear and took a tentative step back into the dining room. "Well, I'll just clear the table for you and go up to bed then."

"You'll do the dishes, too," Tyler informed her.

She stopped. "But I have—"

"A big test tomorrow. I know."

Father and daughter studied each other for a long second. Tyler had the odd feeling he was looking at a stranger. This beautiful young woman couldn't be his little girl, could she? Not when he'd enrolled her in first grade only last week. And wasn't it just yesterday that he'd taken her to buy her first bra? She'd cowered self-consciously behind a rack of clothes while he'd dealt with a saleslady who clearly believed such 'delicate' matters should be left to the girl's mother. Where had the years gone?

"Come and sit down."

The line of her full mouth tightened a fraction. She moved from the doorway to the table and took the chair across from him. "You know you shouldn't be drinking that stuff this late," she commented, glancing at his coffee cup and making a face. "You'll be up all night."

Tyler nearly smiled. Grandma Lou used to tell him the same thing. But he knew his daughter was trying to divert his attention and he stopped the smile from reaching his mouth.

"I've got too much on my mind to sleep," he said.

His daughter gave a resigned sigh. "Dad—"

"You were rude tonight."

Her gaze fell away and she stared at her hands clasped in her lap. "I'm sorry."

"I'm not the one you should be apologizing to."

"I know."

"What the hell's going on, Holly?"

His soft curse had her looking at him again, tears brimming her eyes. Tyler did his darnedest to ignore them. It hadn't been his intention to make her cry—he always lost a piece of his heart when she did. But he wasn't going to apologize either. Not after the stunt she'd pulled.

"I told you," she began, her voice not quite steady, "I had a test."

"You don't even have a class with Mrs. Roberst on Thursdays."

Her gaze dropped.

"Don't lie to me, baby. I can take anything but that."

Tyler saw her brows draw together, the sudden tight set of her mouth. She sat in stony silence. He bit back his frustration.

"I thought we'd talked about this," he said,

Cindy Hiday

keeping his voice low. "It's not like you to act this way."

She looked at him then, her confusion and anger mirrored in her dark eyes, the threat of tears gone. "How am I supposed to act, Dad? All of a sudden I don't feel like this is my home anymore."

Surprised, Tyler asked, "Why would you feel that way?"

"Because you never brought any of the others into our house before. Why now? Why her?"

"Her name is Beth. And what do you mean by 'the others'?"

"Oh, please," Holly said in that do-you-take-me-for-an-idiot tone she had. "I know you dated when Grandma was still alive, because she told me. And later, when you'd have a sitter come over because you were going to be late—" she shrugged, "—I knew it wasn't always because of work."

So much for his attempt at discretion. "How come you never said anything about this before?"

"It didn't matter. *They* didn't matter," she replied, "or you would have brought them home."

Tyler made a mental note to never

underestimate his daughter again. "How'd you get to be so smart?"

"Guess I inherited it from my old man," she grumbled.

Tyler's brow lifted. "Old man?"

"It's a figure of speech, Dad."

Tyler grunted.

"Do you love her? Beth, I mean?"

The question was so unexpected and sudden it took him a few seconds to recover enough to answer. And then it was to admit simply, "I don't know."

If wanting someone so much you felt it like a low-burning fire in your gut, if wanting to know that person inside and out, body and soul, was love, then yes, he supposed it would be safe to say he loved Beth.

But the lady was scared. Too scared to be confronted with words like love and trust and commitment. And he still wasn't completely sure why.

"I'd like the opportunity to get to know her better," he told his daughter. "But if you're going to continue to make her feel unwelcome—"

"I was nervous, all right?" Holly shot to her feet. "Or don't my feelings matter?"

Tyler resisted the oath that hovered on the

tip of his tongue. "Of course your feelings matter to me," he said. "And I hope mine matter to you."

She stared at him, clearly surprised that he would have to ask. "I want you to be happy, Daddy."

"But?"

She turned and walked stiffly to the sink. "What if I don't like Beth?" she asked with her back to him. "What if she doesn't like me?"

"I think if you gave her half a chance, you'd find the two of you have a lot in common."

"But if we don't?"

Tyler raked his fingers through his hair. "I don't know. Then I suppose we'll have to work something out." Although at the moment, he didn't have a clue what that would be.

"Yeah," Holly said roughly, "like send me to college. Then I'll be out of the way."

Tyler gave a heavy sigh that was part relief, part exasperation. "So that's what this is all about."

"Well?" Holly turned and folded her arms in front of her, her chin jutting. "It's the truth, isn't it?"

"No." He stood to get himself another cup of coffee. "It's about as far from the truth as you can get."

"Honest?"

The trace of uncertainty in her voice had him looking at her. That feeling of time as something elusive slipping through his fingers came over him again. It occurred to him just how fragile his relationship with his daughter was, how vulnerable to change.

Was it that same vulnerability that had Beth cursing him? She couldn't stop the inevitable changes his presence in her life would cause, good or bad. But she couldn't shut him out any more than he could her.

He studied his daughter. She isn't nervous, he realized. She's scared. His little girl was facing an uncertain future and she needed to know that at least one thing in her life, his love for her, would remain constant.

"I swear, baby," he told her softly, "my feelings for Beth have nothing to do with you going to college."

"Does that mean I don't have to go then, if I don't want to?" she asked with guarded hope in her voice.

Tyler winked at her over the rim of his cup. "Nice try. Go on up to bed. We'll talk about this some more tomorrow."

"What about the dishes?"

"I'll do them. This time. Besides," he gave a

self-deprecating grin, "I've had too much coffee to sleep."

"Thanks, Daddy." Holly planted a quick kiss on his cheek. But before leaving, she asked, "When are you going to see Beth again?"

"I wish I knew."

~~~

Uttering a sound of disgust, Beth tossed the bedcovers back and sat up. Her head pounded from the futile battle she'd been waging for the past two hours. Try as she might, she could not force herself to go to sleep. Bo Diddley roused from his favorite throw-rug on the floor next to the bed and watched as she pulled her robe on over her chemise.

"It's all right, boy. Go back to sleep."

The big dog sighed and laid his head on his front paws, but when Beth slid her feet into her terry slippers and started for the kitchen, he followed close behind.

Rather than turn on the overhead fluorescent light, Beth used the small light above the sink to find her way around. She tossed Bo a dog biscuit from the box on the counter, bypassing their usual ritual of begging and chastising. She had too many other things on her mind tonight. She poured herself a glass of milk, then found the small bottle of dark coffee liqueur stashed in the cupboard behind an unopened box of pancake mix.

A craving for buttermilk pancakes, dripping with maple syrup, had possessed her to buy the mix weeks ago. But once she'd gotten it home, she'd never found time to actually make the darn things.

You could have made the time.

"Your problem is you're always thinking of yourself," her ex-husband had told her, frequently. "You could at least try to learn how to cook, for my sake. Or don't my feelings mean anything to you?"

Beth gave the cap on the liqueur bottle a savage twist. She *had* tried, damn it. She'd spent hours attempting to put together balanced, edible meals. But her artistic nature had seemed to fall short in the kitchen. And Eric had never missed an opportunity to make her feel guilty for that shortcoming.

Looking back on it now, she could see that her inability had been partly from lack of interest, and partly stubborn resistance to being told what to do and how to act. Eric had claimed to love everything about her, but after they were married, he'd done everything in his power to change her.

Beth poured a generous measure of the

dark, sweet liqueur into her milk and put the cap back on the bottle. Heating milk on the stove without scorching it also seemed to be beyond her. And her one attempt at doing it in the microwave had left her with a curdled mess. She took her hastily made drink to the breakfast bar and scooted onto one of the tall stools. If the alcohol didn't put her to sleep, maybe it would at least take the edge off her restless thoughts.

She gave a short, mirthless laugh that had Bo looking at her with worry in his deep brown eyes. "It's okay," she murmured, once more reassuring him.

But it wasn't okay at all, or she wouldn't be sitting here in semi-darkness, a bundle of sleepless nerves. Tyler had her feeling things, wanting things. Things foreign and exciting and frightening. Even now, remembering his smile, the sound of his easy laughter, the tender way he'd kissed her, sent a warm rush of longing through her. He was growing on her.

He knew it, too.

He'd made it clear his desires were just as strong. More so. But he was looking for something long-term. *A love that lasts a lifetime.* Beth didn't believe such a thing was possible.

She wanted to, but love was an emotion she'd learned not to trust. The past had been a harsh teacher.

Tyler deserved to be loved unconditionally, totally. And he deserved to know why she could never be that someone. He deserved her honesty.

Acting on impulse, Beth moved to the end of the bar and reached for the wall phone. It wasn't until the connection was made and the phone rang once, that she remembered the late hour and started to hang up. But the sound of Tyler's rushed "Hello?" stopped her.

"Hi," she murmured. "Were you sleeping?"

"Beth." The huskiness in his voice had her heart thudding crazily. "I was hoping you'd call."

"Then I didn't wake you?"

His deep-throated chuckle made her skin tingle. "After four cups of coffee, I doubt I'll be getting much sleep tonight."

"Did Holly make it home all right?"

"Yes. Thank you for asking."

"I hope you went easy on her."

"I have the dish-pan hands to prove it," he grumbled good-naturedly.

Beth smiled. "I'm glad."

"Go ahead and laugh," he said, as though he

could feel her smile through the phone line. "It's your turn next time."

Next time. A quick little bolt of fear and anticipation shot through her. "About tonight—"

"The soufflé gave you heartburn."

His remark startled a soft laugh from her. "No, dinner was lovely." She took a determined breath. "If I hide behind my divorce, Tyler, it's a lesson I learned the hard way."

"We don't have to talk about this now, Beth."

It was sweet of him not to push when she knew it was exactly what he wanted. But yes, they did have to talk about it. She did. She had to make him understand. "Eric Wilson was a broker for his father's investment service. We met at a party. He was tall and good looking and intelligent," she said, forcing herself to remember the good as well as the bad. "It was a classic case of love at first sight."

"Did you marry right away?"

"Yes. I wanted to wait until I'd finished college, but he didn't." A chill came over her. "That should have been my first clue things would always have to be his way."

"Is that what caused the marriage to fall apart?"

A thousand images flooded her head, from

her happiness on their wedding day, to her desperate flight five long years later. The bad memories far out-weighed the good. She closed her eyes against them, but it was no use. They'd become permanently etched in her mind. "It was a lot of little things," she said. "I shrugged them off at first. But I think I knew even before our first anniversary that things weren't right."

"Yet you stayed with him."

Desperation formed like a lump in her throat, choking her. How could she possibly explain the shame she'd felt? The feeling that she was somehow the cause of her husband's erratic moods. That maybe she deserved his criticism. That if she just worked harder at it, she could keep the marriage together.

"I wanted to believe that, deep down, he was a good man," she admitted.

"I understand."

The rawness in his voice brought her up short. "You do, don't you?"

"No matter how many times my dad hit me, I wanted to think he really loved me."

Again Beth squeezed her eyes closed, this time against the sharp ache in her heart for the lonely little boy she heard in Tyler's voice. Oh, he tried to hide it, but the pain was still there.

She ached to hold him close and ease the memories that haunted him.

"Eric was much more subtle," she said after a moment, fighting back the nausea that always came with remembering. "If I didn't want to do something he did, he'd accuse me of not loving him enough. He'd tell me he loved me, then criticize everything I did. He'd say demeaning things to me in front of his friends. He took things..." She had to stop and swallow against the helpless rage that filled her throat.

"It's all right, baby," Tyler said softly.

Instead of being offended by the endearment, Beth felt...cherished. His tenderness brought tears to her eyes. She pressed her fingers to the bridge of her nose to block them. "No, it's not all right. He took things he knew were dear to me and destroyed them." She drew in a harsh breath, finding strength in her anger. "When I told him I wanted to finish getting my degree, he was supportive. But then he'd find ways of making me miss my classes, or invite his parents over when he knew I had to study. I finally had to drop out." A harsh, choked sound escaped her. "Would you believe I was grateful to him for being sympathetic? He said it was probably for the best, that I should stay home and learn to cook. I never knew what he was going to say or do next. When Daddy died, he was there for me." She had to stop and take another deep, settling breath. "He helped my mother make all the funeral arrangements," she continued after a moment. "He could be so charming and caring when it served his purpose."

"He manipulated you."

"It was more than manipulation," she said, her taut voice barely above a whisper. "I spent so much time trying to be what he wanted me to be, that after awhile, I didn't know who I was anymore. He stole my identity."

"I'm so sorry, Elizabeth."

"Thank you, but I didn't tell you because I want your sympathy. I want you to understand why I won't be rushed into anything, Tyler. I don't want to hurt you. Or Holly. But I don't want you to expect too much. I'm not looking for a permanent relationship."

"What are you looking for?"

"I'm not sure. I just felt you should know the truth, before we..." *What? What is it you think is going to happen?*

"Make love?" Tyler offered.

Beth sighed. They would be lovers. To

continue denying it was a foolish waste of time. "Yes."

"I meant what I said, Beth. No strings. Question is, do you believe me?"

"I believe you want to believe it's possible."

"Don't you think we owe it to ourselves to find out?"

She gave a resigned laugh. "Has anyone ever told you you're a hopeless optimist?"

"It's how I've survived."

Of course, she thought, looking back on the things he'd told her tonight, of all the times he could have easily let the challenges he'd been faced with beat him down. Only optimism and an unwillingness to give up had gotten him through it.

"We're both survivors, Beth."

"Yes," she said, but at the moment she wouldn't place any bets on surviving what this man would do to her heart.

"Let's take it a day at a time, for now," he suggested.

How could she argue with his simple logic? "Bo and I are going up to Government Camp this Sunday," she told him. "You and Holly are welcome to come along if you'd like."

Originally developed to house the workers who'd built the Timberline Lodge ski resort on

Mount Hood, Government Camp had become a small resort in itself, with sled and ski runs, gift shops and restaurants. It was another one of those historic places Tyler had acquainted himself with, though he didn't get many requests to go there.

"Sounds like fun," he said. But then Beth could have invited him to a Laundromat and he would have accepted if it meant seeing her again. "I'll talk it over with Holly, and make sure Dan can cover for me. I'll call you tomorrow?"

"All right. Good night, Tyler. And thank you again for dinner."

"It was my pleasure."

"Tyler?" she said in a rush, before he could break the connection.

"What is it?"

"You lied when you told me Holly was looking forward to meeting me, didn't you?"

The accusation in her voice hurt. But it was deserved. "Yes. I—"

"Don't ever do that to me again," she said, and hung up.

10

Tyler knew the instant Beth opened her door to him Sunday morning that if he made any mention of the things she'd told him, or tried to comfort her in any way, she would slam it in his face. Pride drew her finely arched brows together. Challenge sparked in her cat-green eyes. In slim-fitting jeans and a soft blue turtleneck sweater, her white snowboots planted shoulder-width apart, she looked fierce and beautiful and so damned vulnerable Tyler was tempted to ignore her defensive posture and haul her into his arms. He ached to quiet her demons, hold her until she realized she couldn't close her heart to him. But the lady needed time to figure it out for herself.

He gave what he hoped was a convincingly

guileless smile. "Ready to go?"

"Where's Holly?"

"She's waiting in the Jeep. I hope you don't mind if I drive."

"What's the matter?" A teasing smile played at the corners of her mouth. "Don't you trust my driving ability?"

"What I don't trust," he replied, casting a side-long glance at her little Geo, "is my ability to get out of that thing, should I be lucky enough to get into it in the first place."

Beth gave his long legs encased in black denim and the broad sweep of his shoulders beneath a bulky gray sweatshirt and sheepskin-lined corduroy jacket a quick once-over. "I see your point. I'll get my things."

"Is there something I can help with?"

Beth grabbed a green wool blanket from a pile of things on the end of the couch and tossed it to him. "Take this to the Jeep for me?"

"Sure, but—"

"It's for Bo. You don't want to see what he can do to your car seat when he's wet."

"Right."

"Change your mind about driving?"

He shot her a dimpled smile that made her pulse shift. "Nope."

"Good." She began tucking her hair into a

white popcorn-knit cap. "I'll be out in a minute."

Tyler and Holly were waiting beside the Jeep when she emerged from the house moments later. She had just enough time to register how alike father and daughter looked standing together in their heavy coats and dark jeans—both tall, one slender where the other was lean, both with that innocent tilt of the nose, one genuine, the other dangerously deceiving. Then she was being dragged off the porch by an eager Bo Diddley. She struggled to keep the straps of her canvas tote from sliding off the shoulder of her thick white parka with one hand while pulling against the shepherd's superior strength with the other.

"Slow down," she scolded. "They aren't going to leave without us."

He went straight to Tyler, his whip of a tail giving Beth's thigh a bruising whack in the process.

"Hey, fella," Tyler reached down to rub the soft hair beneath the dog's ears, "did you miss me?"

Beth caught Holly's frown as the girl realized her dad had been to the unwelcomed dinner guest's home often enough to have befriended the woman's dog. Beth could have gladly kicked Tyler for putting the two of them in this awkward position, but she doubted it would do anything to endear her to Holly. The girl may be upset with her dad, but that didn't mean she'd stand passively by while another woman thumped on him. Instead, Beth put her faith in her four-legged friend to break the ice barrier.

"His name is Bo Diddley," she said.

This made the girl smile in spite of herself. "Bo Diddley...I like that."

At hearing his name, the shepherd swung his attention to Holly. She held her hand out to him. He sniffed it, then gave it a nudge.

Holly looked at Beth. "Is it all right if I pet him?"

"He'll never forgive you if you don't," Beth said, smiling.

Holly stroked the dog's head and neck. "He's so soft," she said, as though surprised.

"He had a bath just yesterday," Beth told her.

"Oh," the girl cooed, "did you get a bath?" Bo turned his sad brown eyes on her, making her laugh.

Beth could have hugged him. But then she'd always known Bo was a charmer.

"Looks like you've made a new friend,"

Tyler said.

"He's a sweetheart," Holly acknowledged.

Father and daughter exchanged a look then and Holly's smile faded. She stuck her hands in her coat pockets and without quite meeting Beth's eyes, said, "About the other night—"

"Let's forget it, shall we?" Beth offered.

"No..." the girl sighed, "...I was rude. I, um, I'm sorry. It's just that I thought—" She stopped, apparently changing her mind about what she'd been going to say, and instead shrugged and muttered, "I'm sorry."

"I accept your apology, Holly."

Tyler reached around and opened the Jeep's passenger-side door. "What do you say we go find some snow?"

Bo jumped into the back seat without waiting for any further invitation. Holly started to climb in after him, but Beth stopped her with a hand to her sleeve.

"I couldn't ask you to sit with him," she said. "He'll try to lay in your lap."

"I don't mind...really."

Something in Holly's expression reminded Beth of Tyler's remark the day he'd rescued her kitchen from certain disaster, that he'd never had time for a dog. Beth realized his daughter wasn't simply being polite by offering to ride with her new-found friend.

Nevertheless, she gave the girl one more chance to change her mind. "If you're sure..."

"I'm sure."

Holly smiled then, the first genuine smile she'd given Beth since they'd met. Beth hadn't realized just how much she'd wanted the young woman's acceptance until that moment. She felt like shouting for joy. She looked at Tyler and he winked. Beth laughed lightly and let him help her get settled in the front seat.

~~~

The Jeep's tires hummed on the four-lane highway as they left the city behind. The four-wheel drive's stiff suspension rode rough and wind whistled around the vinyl top, but the heater kept them toasty. Beth realized it wouldn't have mattered what Tyler drove. She felt safe with him behind the wheel. She'd made this trip so many times in the past with just Bo for company, it was nice to sit back and let somebody else do the driving for a change.

Tyler's raven-black hair was all but covered by a navy stocking cap, drawing attention to the rest of his striking profile. There was strength and gentleness in the handsome planes and angles of his features. It wasn't just his driving she was comfortable with, Beth decided. He'd read her feelings and respected them. He hadn't pushed or demanded or made her feel inadequate. She didn't know how long it would last, didn't dare hope it would, but for now she accepted it.

It began to snow lightly when they reached the Welches Road intersection, twelve miles from their destination. They approached the turnoff to Beth's vacation home on East Woodsey Ridge Avenue. The small, one-bedroom bungalow high on the south bank of the Sandy River had been in her family for as far back as Beth could remember. She and her parents had spent Christmases there, watching it snow from the big picture window, building snowmen on the deck and sipping hot cocoa in front of the fireplace. Beth still made time every year to bring Bo Diddley up and enjoy the solitude and happy memories. Her mother had joined her once, but the memories had been too hard for her, reminding her of her beloved, departed husband.

A cloud of sadness shadowed Beth's heart. She had her unwelcome memories, as well. The house had been her haven the night she'd left Eric. It was the only place she'd felt safe.

When Tyler drove past the turnoff, Beth started to point it out to him, but something stopped her, a feeling she couldn't identify. Bo sat up in the back seat and whimpered, his haunches wiggling.

Beth shot him a quick glance over her shoulder. "Quiet."

"Is something wrong?" Holly asked. "Does he need to go out and, you know, do something?"

"No," Beth said, staring straight ahead, "he's just eager to play in the snow."

"It won't be long now," Tyler promised.

Highway 26 narrowed to two lanes, forcing the steady, resort-bound traffic to slow. Fat snowflakes drifted to earth as if suspended in slow motion, floating, then clinging. The tall conifers of the Mount Hood National Forest—pine, fir, spruce and cedar—began to look like flocked Christmas trees, the surrounding peaks and slopes of the Cascade Range serene beneath an ethereal blanket of white.

"What are you thinking about?" Tyler's voice, deep and sensual, broke into her thoughts.

"I've been away too long," she answered on a sigh.

"Did you come here often?"

"Yes," she allowed softly. "I'd forgotten how peaceful the mountain could be."

The instant the words were out of her mouth, a bright yellow sports car raced up on their left and darted into the narrow space between the Jeep and the van they'd been following. Tyler hit the brakes, causing the Jeep to fish-tail on the road's snow-slick surface. He pulled the steering wheel in the direction of the skid and quickly regained control of the vehicle, only to lose control of his temper by loudly voicing his opinion of the driver's parentage.

"Daddy!"

Bo made a rumbling sound deep in his throat.

"Easy, boy," Beth commanded, her own voice deliberately calm.

"What's wrong with him?" Holly asked.

"He feels threatened by strong language." Beth slanted Tyler an accusing look.

A nerve ticked in his jaw, his eyes focused on the road. "I'll try to remember that," he grumbled. Then he glanced over at her and Beth could see the tension had already begun to ease from his face.

"Got a bar of soap on you?" he asked.

"Soap?"

"To wash my mouth out with."

"I'm sure I can come up with something."

Tyler chuckled warily at the wicked glint in her eyes. He had a hunch he wasn't going to have to wait long to find out what that something was.

A few minutes later, he signaled and steered the Jeep into the east parking area of Government Camp, finding a vacant slot close to the snow-covered slopes and public restrooms. They all piled out, with Bo doing his best to be first.

Tyler was tugging at the zipper on his coat when a snowball smacked him in the side of the head, knocking his cap askew. Holly let out a peal of laughter. Tyler shot her a playful scowl over the roof of the Jeep before he spotted Beth grinning and calmly packing another snowball between her mittened hands.

"You'd better defend yourself," she warned.

"Why you—" Tyler laughed and took off around the front of the Jeep.

Beth half screamed, half laughed when she realized his intentions. She tried to dodge out of his way and tripped over her clunky boots. He caught her in a tackle and they landed in the snowbank at the edge of the parking lot, with Tyler on top of her.

In that instant, Beth knew what it would be like when he made love to her, the weight of him on her thighs and stomach, his thick black hair wild and unruly as he looked down at her, the flush of his face and the shameless gleam in his smoke-gray eyes. The devil was in those eyes.

"That's a pretty good right arm you've got there," he said, his voice low and far too aware. Then he pressed his cold lips to the corner of her mouth.

"Holly—" Beth began.

"Is chasing Bo across the lot. Remind me to buy him something special for Christmas."

Before Beth could respond, Tyler shifted his weight and helped her to her feet.

She spotted Bo Diddley immediately, bounding toward them and dragging his leash with a mitten caught in it.

"Hey!" Holly shouted, running after him and waving a bare hand.

Beth's eyes widened. "Watch out!"

But her warning came too late.

Tyler was sure a freight train had plowed into him when he found himself laying face first in the snow, the wind knocked out of him and what felt like a hundred pounds of dog standing on his back. Before there was time to register fear, Bo began slathering a smooth wet tongue across Tyler's ear and the side of his face.

"Bo, down!" he heard Beth command.

The weight lifted and Tyler rolled onto his back, eyes closed, arms outstretched. He groaned, pretending to be hurt. Soft snowflakes lit and melted on his face. Seconds ticked by. When no tender hands arrived to minister to his make-believe pain, he opened his eyes a slit and peered up. Beth stood over him on his right, Holly at his left. They each had a snowball in hand and were exchanging grins. Realizing his impending plight, Tyler grabbed an ankle in each hand and yanked. Holly and Beth squealed and stumbled back, giving him time to clamber to his feet.

The next several minutes were a blur of frozen crystals and laughter as the three of them threw hastily packed snowballs at each other. Bo barked and leaped to catch the snowy missiles in flight, only to have them explode in his face.

"Time!" Beth yelled. Tyler threw another snowball and she ducked, laughing. "I give!"

He moved in and swung her off her feet in a hug that made him stagger in the ankle deep snow. She opened her mouth to protest and he kissed her. His lips were almost numb from cold, but feeling returned with languorous ease. When he drew back to look at her, her cheeks were flushed and the secret worries that usually creased her brow were gone. Tyler silently vowed to do everything in his power to see that look on her face more often.

"What?" she asked with a hesitant smile.

He shook his head. "Nothing. You just look happy."

"I am." The admission surprised a laugh out of her. She met the warmth in his intent gaze. Because of you, she thought. She considered telling him, but decided from the look in his eyes, he'd already figured it out.

Bo barked and the moment was gone. Beth looked around and saw Holly chasing the big dog again and laughing each time he succeeded in dodging her moves.

"How come he didn't take my head off when I tackled you?" Tyler asked.

"He didn't sense any fear from me." That's what surprised her the most, she decided. Tyler didn't have any hidden agendas. His feelings were right there in his eyes.

She smiled and moved out of his arms. "Let's go rent some innertubes."

It stopped snowing and the sun filtered through a thinning layer of clouds. Tyler, Beth and Holly shared the long snow-packed slope that began high in the trees and ended at the parking lot with a swarm of other people, adults and children alike, who had come to the mountain for a day of fun. They each took turns staying below with Bo, so he wouldn't get in the way of careening innertubers and wild sledders.

Two hours later, exhausted and soaked, Beth and Holly escaped to the women's restroom to change. A wooden bench ran the length of the wall across from a row of stalls and sinks. Beth dropped onto it with a tired sigh and began pulling at the laces of her rubber boots.

Holly sat next to her and unlaced her own boots. "This was fun," she said. "Thank you for inviting me."

"You're welcome. I hope Bo wasn't too much of a pest."

"He's terrific." The young woman pulled off first one boot, then the other. "You really like my dad, don't you?"

Caught off guard by the question, Beth took time to remove a damp sock and begin vigorously rubbing her cold toes between her hands before answering. "What makes you ask?"

Holly shrugged. "I've never like seen him

kiss somebody that way before."

"Oh." So much for discretion. Beth felt her face warm. "I, um, don't know what to say."

"That's okay. I think it's kind of...romantic." Holly's mouth tipped in a crooked smile that emulated her father's. "Weird," she continued, "but romantic."

Beth laughed. "I couldn't have said it better." Tyler was probably the most romantic man she'd ever met, and he left her feeling weird inside.

"So, do you?" Holly asked. "Like him, I mean?"

"Yes," Beth replied cautiously, testing the feel of it, then clarified, "I like being with him."

Holly stood to wiggle out of her damp leggings, her brows pulled into a small frown, as though uncertain whether or not she was comfortable with Beth's answer.

"Holly, I'd be the last person to try to come between you and your dad," Beth told her. "I was very close to my father, too, so I think I understand how you're feeling."

Holly pushed her long legs into a dry pair of light gray sweatpants and sat down to don clean socks. "Can I ask you something?"

"Sure."

"Did your dad make you go to college?"

Beth smiled. "My parents didn't have much luck making me do anything I didn't want to do." She stood and wiggled out of her wet jeans. "College was my choice. I felt a degree in Fine Arts would give me a better understanding of design and lend credibility to my profession." She dug through her canvas tote for a pair of jeans. "Why do you ask?"

"Dad wants me to go to college."

"But you don't?"

"I don't know." She shoved her foot into a chunky black leather shoe. "I mean, why waste my time if I'm not sure what I want to do with my life?"

"There are community colleges," Beth suggested, sitting to put on her socks and shoes. "You could take a few classes in things that interest you until you found something you wanted to stick with."

"Tell my dad that." She yanked on the laces of her shoes so hard Beth expected them to snap.

"That's something you need to do, Holly."

"He won't listen to me. He already has his mind made up."

"He just wants you to have the things he didn't."

"I know," Holly replied with a sigh. "But I'm

not my dad."

Beth considered informing her that she was more like Tyler than she realized, but decided against it. It wasn't her place. Besides, what did she know about giving a teenager advice?

Still, past experience compelled her to say, "Your dad loves you, Holly, but if you don't want to go to college, you need to tell him that. It's your life, after all. You have to stand up for yourself."

Beth was painfully aware of the consequences of trying to live by someone else's rules, but she couldn't shake the sudden panic feeling in her stomach that she'd just jumped into the middle of something she'd have been better off staying out of.

"Thanks, Beth."

"For what?"

"For being honest with me and not treating me like a child." Again she sighed, her eyes stopping just short of meeting Beth's. "Especially after I acted like one."

"You're hardly a child, Holly. As for the rest, you're welcome." Beth stood and grabbed her bulging tote. "We'd better get going before your dad sends in a search party."

On the way home, they ordered double burgers, fries and hot fudge sundaes at the

Dairy Queen's drive-thru in Rhododendron. Beth ordered a small dish of plain ice cream for Bo so Holly could eat without having to endure his begging looks. And she helped Tyler with his food so he could keep at least one hand free to drive. She'd never realized how erotic feeding a man French fries, one at a time, could be. Especially when he deliberately took the whole fry in his mouth to suck the ends of her fingers.

It was early afternoon when they pulled into her driveway. Holly said her good-byes, then moved to the front seat to wait while Tyler walked Beth to the door. Bo trotted ahead and was standing by the gate at the side of the house, waiting to be let into his yard.

"You and Holly seem to be hitting it off," Tyler remarked.

"She's a lovely young woman." Beth opened the gate and Bo began a methodical sweep of the ground with his nose. "What's not to like about her?"

"I'll tell her you said that."

Beth gave him a small frown as she pulled the gate closed. "Did I miss something?"

"I'll explain later."

"I'll bet you have your hands full with the boys." Beth started for the house.

"Not really." Tyler walked behind her slightly, enjoying the tantalizing sway of hips in denim. "Holly's always been taller than most of the boys her age. The teenage male ego finds that hard to deal with."

"She won't be a teenager much longer." Beth shot him a smile over her shoulder. "And the boys will catch up."

"Don't remind me."

"I wouldn't worry." They reached the porch and she dug a key out of her zippered coat pocket. "I have the feeling she's intelligent enough to make the right choices—about a lot of things." She looked away to fit the key in the lock.

It was the last part of her statement that caught Tyler's attention. "What did the two of you talk about up there on the mountain?"

"What makes you ask?"

"I know my daughter. She's had that look on her face, like she's getting ready to spring something on me."

Beth pushed the door open and met his gaze. "Maybe you should talk to her."

"Meaning you're not going to tell me. I am her father, Beth. If it's something I should know about—"

"And I'm someone she's just met," Beth

interrupted, her tone kind but firm. "It's not my place to speak for her."

Tyler felt an unfamiliar arrow of jealousy that he quickly suppressed. Other than the occasional advice from one of her friends or that friend's mother, Holly hadn't had a stable female influence in her life since Grandma Lou's death. If she was comfortable confiding in Beth, he had no reason to deny her that.

"You're right. Forget I brought it up."

"I understand your concern, Tyler. It can't be easy raising a teenager these days."

"It takes a lot of patience." He lifted his hand then to touch her cheek. "Like any relationship," he continued, his voice lowering.

"Why do I have the feeling yours is about to run out?" she whispered.

"It's never been one of my strong points." He pulled his hand back and drew in a rough breath. "I need to be with you, Beth—without Holly or Bo or Sam around."

"You could always come in for that tattoo."

His mouth twisted into a grimace. "Thanks, but I've been through enough pain to last me awhile."

Beth laughed. "I have to admit, that double somersault you did off the innertube was very impressive. And your scream almost had me convinced you really were in agony."

"I'll be sitting carefully for a few days."

She lifted a hand to his face, traced a finger around his ear, saw his gray eyes darken. "It would be a shame if you got hurt," she softly admitted. Her fingers swept the heavy pulse at the side of his neck, then curled into the soft sheepskin collar of his coat. "I had a nice time today, Tyler. Thank you."

"The pleasure was mine," he murmured. "When can I see you again?"

"Sam and I are going Christmas shopping this evening. You're welcome to come along."

"That's not what I need and you know it."

Yes, she knew. She needed the same thing. She became very still as he drew his fingers across her lips.

"I can be patient a while longer," he told her. "On one condition."

"What's that?"

"Convince me this isn't the last time I'll see you."

Beth swallowed, her own pulse leaping. "How?"

He stepped forward, backing her against the doorjamb. "Use your imagination."

Beth's cheeks warmed. "Your daughter's watching."

"She's seen us kiss."

"Yes, I know. Is that all you want?"

"You know better."

Beth's face burned. "Good grief, don't you ever think of anything else?"

"Not lately. Lady, you are driving me crazy."

Beth realized she liked that, knowing she could have that effect on him. She gave him a smile bordering on sinful.

"Sanity is highly over-rated," she whispered and wrapped her arms around his neck. She had to stand on tiptoe to reach his mouth. He wasn't going to make it easy for her by meeting her half way. He needed reassurance.

And he would have it.

She nipped at his lower lip, then lightly ran the tip of her tongue across the spot. He drew in a sharp breath and she took advantage, feeling his soft, wordless sound of need caress her lips, the rough velvet of his tongue as he returned her kiss. He circled her waist and drew her tighter. The constraint of clothes between them was frustrating. Beth clenched her fingers in his hair and focused on his mouth, the taste that was his alone, the promise of sensuality that sent a sweet ache through her.

She drew away slowly, unwilling to let him

go. "Convinced yet?"

"Lady, any more convinced and I'm sending Holly home without me."

11

"Oh look!" Sammy grabbed Beth's arm and propelled her toward one of the display windows in the mall. "Isn't that blazer fabulous?"

"It would look great on you," Beth acknowledged, unable to hide her weariness.

She and Sam had been shopping for two hours and all she had to show for it were tired feet. The novelty of seeing the Christmas decorations that adorned the shops had worn out by the time they'd circled both levels of Lloyd Center Mall, twice. She should have forgone fashion and worn her sneakers, instead of the pumps that complemented her black Capri-length leggings and floral-print tunic.

Her gift list was short—her mother, Samantha, Marie, and Anthony, the young man at Quick Clips who did his best to unfrazzle her hair once a month. But instead, Beth found herself shopping for Tyler. A frustrating endeavor. Everything she'd considered was either too personal, or not personal enough. It might have been easier if she knew just how personal she wanted to get. He'd made it very clear that he wanted her, in every sense of the word. And she'd as much as admitted to him she wanted the same thing. She'd said and done a lot of things lately that went against her better judgment. When he held her, kissed her, seduced her with his sexy dimples and heart-stopping eyes, better judgment was the furthest thing from her mind.

Maybe she could find a nice place to hide until the holidays were over.

She cast a side-long glance at Sam, who looked depressingly unruffled in a lime silk blouse tucked into stone-washed jeans, and a comfortable pair of running shoes. Two huge shopping bags hung from her arm.

"I thought we were shopping for gifts," Beth grumbled.

"There's nothing wrong with buying myself

a gift, is there?"

Beth shrugged. "Of course not. It's your money."

"Besides, how do you know I wasn't thinking of getting it for *you*?"

Beth eyed the salmon-pink blazer and shuddered at the thought of what it would look like next to her red hair and light complexion. "It'll be the last thing you ever buy me."

"You're no fun."

"Sorry." Beth sighed. "I'd be more fun if I could sit down for a few minutes."

"Played too hard this morning, heh?"

"I had a good time," Beth replied, avoiding the tell-me-more look in her friend's expression. She'd had a wonderful time, darn it. Warmth curled through her remembering. Being with Tyler and Holly had made her feel wanted and needed and just a little reckless. In fact, she'd never felt this compelled toward recklessness before. It had her wound as tight as a child's play toy, ready to fly apart at the slightest touch.

It didn't help that Christmas was ten days away and she didn't have a single gift to wrap, she thought irritably. She shifted her trenchcoat to the other arm and glanced at her watch. "The stores aren't going to close for awhile yet. Let's go find a cup of coffee."

"Something with chocolate in it," Sam said decisively.

Beth cast her a disparaging look. "Is there any other kind?"

They discovered they weren't the only ones with a caffeine pick-me-up in mind as they shuffled through a sea of people in the coffee shop and placed their order. A short while later, double mochas in hand, Sam spotted an empty bench in the center of the mall and they rushed to lay claim to it. Beth groaned in pleasure as she sat back and sipped the hot, strong liquid, thick with whipped milk and chocolate sprinkles.

"So, how did it go this morning?" Sam asked. "Did you and Tyler's daughter get along all right?"

"Bo did most of the charming," Beth admitted with a tired chuckle. "But, yes, we seemed to hit it off." She paused to take another sip of coffee, her brows pulling together. "She's a confused young woman, Sam. Her father's determined she go to college, but she's not sure what she wants to do."

"She told you this?"

"I know, it seemed odd to me, too. I mean,

she barely knows me."

"Maybe she just needed somebody impartial to talk to," Sam suggested. "What did you say to her?"

Beth cringed. "I told her not to let anyone make her decisions for her."

"Do you think that was wise?"

"How should I know?" Beth's impatience spilled into her voice. "I've never done this kind of thing before. But she seemed to want my honest opinion. So, right or wrong, I told her how I felt."

"How do you think Tyler's going to react?"

An all-too-familiar flutter of apprehension settled uneasily in Beth's stomach. How many times during her marriage had she asked herself that same question about Eric after she'd said or done something without consulting him first? How many times had she let it eat at her to the point of being afraid to say or do anything?

"I'm sure he'll understand," she said.

But she wasn't sure. Not really. She wanted to believe Tyler would be fair and take Holly's feelings into consideration. She wanted to believe he was nothing like Eric. But she also knew how strongly he felt about his daughter getting the education he'd never had. Would he force his will on Holly, convinced it was the best thing for her, whether she liked it or not?

Beth shook the troubling thought from her head. "Holly's probably blowing the whole thing out of proportion," she said, more for her own benefit than Sammy's. "I'll have a talk with Tyler the next time I see him. In the meantime," she downed the last of her coffee and checked her watch, "we have some serious shopping to do."

~~~

Beth didn't see Tyler in the days that followed. He didn't call. He didn't drop by unannounced, at her house or the studio. She realized just how much she'd grown to expect his sudden appearances. She missed them. She missed him—his spontaneity, his touch, the sound of his laughter. He'd warned her that patience wasn't one of his strong points, and yet he didn't seem to have a problem keeping his distance now. As one day slid into another, Beth began to wonder if he was having second thoughts. Had a few days apart made him realize his feelings for her weren't as strong as he'd believed?

The possibility left her feeling at odds with herself. She'd resisted an involvement with him from day one. But her heart, it seemed, had turned a deaf ear. It was too late to think saying good-bye wouldn't hurt, that she could walk away from Tyler Stone without regrets.

All of a sudden her work at the studio didn't bring her the satisfaction it once had. She found her mind wandering at the most inopportune moments, her ability to focus all but nonexistent. She'd never been much of a daydreamer, but lately that was all she seemed to do. Marie had had to remind her twice to return Dr. Rivers's calls, and Sam had caught her gazing out the window, when she should have been prepping for the patient who'd been waiting in the outer office for almost thirty minutes.

But it was the dreams she had while asleep that had her both anticipating and dreading going to bed every night. Vivid and sensuous, she'd awaken damp with sweat, her heart pounding a mad rhythm in her chest, her senses heightened to such a degree that she was certain her body would spontaneously combust at the slightest spark. Morning after morning, she stumbled out of bed frustrated, unsatisfied, and so cranky that even Bo began to keep his distance.

By Saturday morning, she was a wreck.

"This is ridiculous," she muttered, staring at

her pathetic reflection in the bathroom mirror. Dark circles shadowed her eyes, her hair was impossibly tangled, and she was exhausted. She couldn't call the night she'd just had restful by any stretch of the imagination. Images of a great white steed and its tall, dark rider charging through a wall of flames, a strong hand sweeping her to safety, the flight of the phoenix beneath her and the solid, heated flesh of the magnificent male in her arms as they kissed, caressed, plunged, then floated, arms and legs entwined...

Beth groaned at the sudden flush that warmed her skin from her hairline down to the lace of her chemise and beyond. She always woke up before she and the mystical horseman made love. Night after night, her dream brought her frustratingly close, so close that when she woke she imagined she could still feel his touch on her skin. His scent still lingered on the bed sheets. Longing plagued her like a toothache.

"Just call him," she growled at her reflection. Then before she could talk herself out of it, she marched to her bedroom, snatched the handset from the phone on the nightstand and punched in the number Tyler had written on the back of his business card.

Holly answered. "Hello?"

"Hi, Holly. This is Beth."

"Oh, hi," the girl replied, her tone cheery. "I'm glad you called."

Beth became instantly wide awake. "You are?"

"Yeah. I've been wanting to thank you again for your advice last weekend. It really helped."

Beth gave a relieved sigh. "You've talked with your dad."

"No," there was the briefest hesitation, then, "but I'm going to, soon."

"That's good, Holly." Beth tried to sound more confident than she felt. But the apprehension that had been eating at her had returned. She lifted the base of the phone from the nightstand and paced beside the bed. "I'm sure you'll work something out," she said determinedly. "Is your dad there?"

"No, he's got clients all day. I can give you his cell-phone number."

"That's okay," Beth replied. "I have it here."

"Dad and I are going out tomorrow to get a Christmas tree. Do you think you and Bo could come with?"

Beth smiled, touched by the girl's gesture. "It's nice of you to invite us, Holly. I'll talk it over with your dad."

They said their good-byes and Beth set the phone down to punch in Tyler's business number.

"Luxury Coach Services. Tyler Stone speaking."

The sound of his deep, velvet-edged voice washed through Beth like warm pudding. She abruptly sat on the edge of the bed before her legs could give out.

"It's me," she murmured.

"Beth."

The surprise and pleasure in the breathless way he spoke her name sang in her heart. "I hear traffic. Am I interrupting?"

"No. I've got a few minutes before my clients are ready to go. Is anything wrong?"

I miss you. "I'm going to Juliet's tonight," she said, grabbing at the first idea that came into her head. "They're having a big Christmas party, two-for-one drinks, a live band." The words tumbled from her in an effort to keep up with her brain, already two steps ahead. What would she wear? Could Anthony squeeze her into his schedule? But more importantly, could Tyler? And did he want to? She forced her racing thoughts to shift into neutral and drew in a deep, steadying breath. "Can you meet me there after work?"

"I won't be free until ten. Is that too late?"

It took her a second to respond. She'd almost convinced herself he'd say no, that the whole idea had been crazy. But the only crazy thing at the moment was the way her pulse was dancing over itself. "Ten would be fine. I'll see you then."

~~~

Tyler ignored the disgruntled looks he got as he pushed his way to the entrance of Juliet's. He was late. He'd called his daughter, told her not to wait up for him, then stopped at the market. Traffic had been hell. If Beth had given up on him—

"Hey, Tyler!" Samantha greeted him just inside the heavy wooden door, shouting to be heard over the din of music and conversation emanating from the room behind her. "It's good to see you again!"

She sounded like she had a headcold because of the red foam ball stuck to the end of her nose. Stuffed felt antlers perched on her head and a collar with tiny silver bells dangling from intermittent points along its hem, "Rudolf" embossed at an angle in white, completed the costume.

Tyler gave a polite, albeit distracted, nod. "Hi, Sam!" His throat felt like eighty-grit sandpaper. "Is she here?"

Sammy gave a knowing smile and jabbed a thumb over her shoulder. "Go on in!"

Red and green streamers with candy canes and mistletoe hung from the rafters of the singles' nightclub. Waiters and waitresses wore red felt vests and Santa hats with cotton tassels, and a five piece band played a jazzy rendition of *Christmas Ball Blues*. Tyler scanned the semi-darkened room, wondering where to start. The wall of people seemed to go on forever, couples exchanging seductive glances, gesturing, signaling, inviting. A smokescreen of fragrances assaulted his senses.

Suddenly every nerve ending came alive. She was across the dance floor, talking to a young man in a University of Oregon sweater, her head tipped slightly as though hanging on his every word, her hands wrapped around the stem of a wine glass. Her hair was swept up in some loose style that exposed her delicate neck, the smooth slope of her shoulders. She wore a sleeveless black sequined number that seemed to defy gravity as it hugged her firm, rounded breasts, her small waist, and the gentle curve of her hips, then came to an abrupt end high on her shapely thighs.

Tyler's body tightened. He couldn't blame

the college kid for wanting to be close to her, but that didn't prevent the urge to grab the pup by the scruff of the neck and toss him on his preppy butt. Beth was *his* woman. It was a primitive reaction, the instinct to possess, one he knew she would rebel against, but he couldn't deny its existence.

Then he realized that the angle of her head allowed her to discreetly look at the door without being rude to her companion. Her cat-green eyes met his and the room shifted beneath his feet.

Beth had been afraid he'd changed his mind. It was almost ten-thirty and she'd spent the last twenty minutes trying to concentrate on the young man who'd offered to buy her another drink and asked her to dance. She'd declined both. He was nice looking enough, but there was only one man she was interested in.

And he'd just walked through the door.

"Excuse me," she murmured and handed her glass to the confused boy as she brushed past him.

Her heart beat rapidly in her throat. She met Tyler in the middle of the crowded dance floor. His hair was mussed, his tie gone and the collar of his shirt open. He looked tired. She slid her hands inside his loose jacket and around his waist. He pulled her into his arms.

"Traffic—" he began, bringing his husky voice close to her ear. His warm breath sent a delicious shiver through her.

"It's all right," she told him and laid her head on his shoulder. The heavy drum of his heart against her ear kept time with hers.

They moved to *That Old Christmas Moon*, their bodies fluid, fitting together as male and female were designed to. Other dancers crushed against them, but Beth ignored them, lost in the man enfolding her, the feel of solid muscle, his subtle woodsy scent heady. His hands slowly roamed her back, her sides, her hips, as if committing her to memory.

"You feel good," he said.

She smiled against the soft fabric of his shirt. "So do you." She didn't know if he heard her. And it didn't matter. Cocooned in his heat, she knew no man had ever stirred her the way Tyler did. She gave into the feeling. She wondered why she'd tried so hard to resist it before.

Tyler had courted risk all his life, but it had been a long time since he'd left himself open to real hurt. The woman in his arms had hurt him by making him wait all week to hear from her. She'd done that to him twice now. But holding her, feeling her body curve into his, he knew he'd gladly go through hell's fire for her.

He'd lost his heart to her. His body's reaction was immediate and physical as they swayed to the music, the raw desire that washed through him exquisite torture. She drew closer, molding her soft mound against the hard ache in his groin. Heat tightened every muscle in his body.

"You're playing with fire again," he warned, his lips brushing the shell of her ear.

Beth lifted her head and met the sharp steel of need in his eyes. It was a look she could identify with. She stood on her toes to bring her mouth close. This time she wanted to make sure he did hear her.

"I want to do more than just play," she told him.

Her heart bumped once hard against her chest at the awareness that flared his nostrils an instant before the pressure of his mouth on hers forced her head back. The music disappeared. The other dancers. Their movements became a seduction in the middle of the dance floor. He kissed her with a hunger matched only by her own.

His hands moved to her hips, molding her to him. "This is how much I want you," he said, clearly not giving a damn if anyone else saw or heard. "This is what you do to me, Beth." He gave her another long, drugging kiss. "Tell me you want me just as much," he demanded, his voice a rough plea.

The naked vulnerability in his face, the magnitude of his desire, frightened and thrilled her. "I do, Tyler." Again she raised up on tiptoe, this time to kiss his throat and the line of his jaw. The man was frustratingly tall. "I do want you," she whispered, then gently bit his earlobe.

Tyler shuddered. He'd waited weeks to hear her say it. A lifetime. He gathered her up and headed her toward the door. "Let's get the hell out of here."

Sam might have said something to them when they stopped long enough for Beth to collect her purse and coat, but Tyler was beyond the point of making any sort of intelligible small talk. As he helped her with her coat, his gaze fell on the phoenix at her back. Tonight he felt like that fabled bird, his life about to change, take flight. He pressed his lips to it, felt Beth's shiver of awareness, a moment before pulling the coat up over her shoulders.

The limousine was double parked in Juliet's

lot. Beth slid across the wide front seat and leaned into the curve of Tyler's arm when he climbed behind the wheel and started driving. She didn't ask where they were going. She didn't care. She was aware only of the maelstrom of emotions pulling at her, and the tall dark man at her side. His profile was harsh in the stark headlights of passing traffic, his features chiseled as though battling his own storm, as though control and sanity were so much dust tossing in the winter wind. The limousine's heater purred softly. Beth closed her eyes and laid her head on Tyler's shoulder, content to ride out the storm with him.

He lost her. Somewhere they'd left the city behind and started climbing. Climbing out of the world. Time passed, but she had no concept of how much. She felt caught on the edge of a dream. The sleek pearl limousine became a powerful white horse charging through the night.

When it seemed as though they could go no higher without dropping over the edge of existence, Tyler pulled the long car off the road and parked. The spot was secluded and quiet. Beth didn't recognize it. A panoramic view of the city spread out below them, a blanket of stars draped above them.

"It's beautiful," she said softly.

"I used to come here when things got too rough at home," he told her, his voice husky and distant. "I'd sit for hours, over there," he pointed to a large rock with a flat surface, "and stare at the lights. Or I'd lay on my back and gaze at the stars."

She knew without asking, could hear it in his voice, that he hadn't been very old, still a boy with a heart that had been broken too many times. She could imagine him out here alone, scared and hurting. A rage like she'd felt only one other time in her life settled bitter and hard in her stomach, a rage so intense it frightened her.

"Where are your parents now?" she asked with forced calm.

"In hell, I hope."

The cold contempt in his words brought her head up sharply. His profile was set in granite, his mouth grim. Beth's heart broke for him. She lifted a hand to his face and cupped his cheek.

"So much pain," she said on a choked breath, swallowing against the tears she knew he would resent.

He looked at her. Torment and longing lay naked in his eyes. "It's nothing to what I feel when I look at you."

Beth's heart stopped, then raced.

Tyler took her hand from his face and pressed his lips to the curve of her wrist. Her skin was warm and soft, the erratic rhythm of her pulse against his mouth stirring an immediate response too graphic to deny. "I was afraid you wouldn't call."

"I didn't want to," she admitted, her voice a breathless whisper. "I didn't want to feel this way."

He knew. Still, it hurt, just a little, hearing her say it aloud. "Tell me how you feel, Beth. I need to know."

Hungry. She'd decided the only way to get him out of her system was to have him, satisfy the craving that plagued her, until it—he—was no longer a craving. But being here with him now, she doubted the sanity of her logic. It would take her a very long time to get over the yearnings that beat inside her.

His lips teased the curve of her wrist once more, a warm whisper against the sensitive area, but his gaze remained locked to hers, waiting.

"I feel..." her breath caught, then rushed from her, "...like I'm going to explode if you don't touch me. Touch me, Tyler."

His eyes darkened. "I'll touch you any way

you want me to. Tell me what you want."

"I want it all. I want you. Now."

She'd asked for the easiest thing in the world. "I'm yours," he said simply. He wondered if she knew just how much a part of him she'd become. He brought his lips down to brush hers lightly, drawing back when she would have pressed closer. Like her, he wanted it all. He was aware of the signals her body was sending, and of how ready his was to comply, how quickly the heat that existed between them could consume. But he was determined to go slowly, savor every moment, every sensation. He didn't want the flame to burn itself out in a hot flash. Given his way, this would not be a one-nighter, but the beginning of the rest of their lives together.

Gently pushing her coat back, he bent his head to the pulse in her neck, felt her skin shiver against his lips when he pressed them to the junction of her collarbone, felt her fingers curl into the front of his shirt as he nipped at her shoulder. "Have I told you how beautiful you are tonight?" he murmured.

"No." Her breathy reply whispered against his ear.

"That dress..." He stopped for lack of words adequate to describe what seeing her in tight black sequins did to him, opting instead to kiss the spot on her shoulder he'd bitten.

"What about my dress?" Her voice had taken on a teasing tone that made him lift his head and look at her. Her green eyes sparkled in the pale light.

Tyler felt the corner of his mouth lift. "I like it."

Beth found it impossible not to return his disarming smile. "I'm glad." She thought of telling him she'd bought it just for him, but didn't. She'd felt giddy and nervous and ridiculous trying on outfit after outfit, looking for the perfect one, the one that would make him see her and no one else. She'd wanted to affect him the way he did her.

She realized she was still clutching his shirt. Her fingers slowly loosened and spread across his chest, absorbing his heat through the rumpled fabric. She watched, mesmerized, as her hands rose and fell with the rhythm of his breathing, tested the muscles of his biceps, brushed her palms over the hard points of his nipples, heard his quick intake of breath. His fingers curled around her wrists and she looked up. He wasn't smiling anymore. His smoke-gray eyes were absolutely predatory.

"I meant what I said, Beth." His voice had

become low and thick. "No games. If you're having any second thoughts—"

"I've never been more sure of anything in my life."

She said it without hesitation, without breaking eye contact. He gave her a kiss that drew the air from her lungs. "We'll have more privacy in back."

Beth nodded.

They moved to the rear of the limousine. Tyler pressed a button on the overhead control panel to raise the partition between the two sections and enclose them in shadowed velvet. Another button provided soft illumination.

Removing her coat, Beth sank back in the plush seat across from him and took in every detail of the moment—the beads of moisture on the unopened bottle of champagne nesting in a bucket of ice, the sweet raspberry fragrance of a single lilac rose in a crystal vase over the bar, the quiet sough of Tyler's uniform, the way the charcoal fabric hinted at his perfect arms and legs and back, and the exquisitely agonizing deliberateness of his movements. She hugged herself to withstand the shock of longing that danced over her skin and realized with sudden clarity the impact this evening, this man, would have on her.

He saw her guarded pose and asked, "Are you cold?" Without waiting for an answer, he shrugged out of his jacket, and sitting next to her, draped it over her shoulders.

It carried his heat, his scent, as if he'd physically wrapped himself around her. Beth closed her eyes and drowned in the sensation.

Tyler drew her into the hollow of his shoulder. She could feel the tight constraint in his body, the price he paid for simply holding her.

"What are you afraid of, Beth?" His words brushed the hair at her temple, sending a shiver over her.

I'm afraid of falling in love with you, her heart cried. She met the magnetic pull of his eyes and her defenses crumbled.

"Losing control," she told him finally. For her, they were one in the same.

"I promise—"

"Don't," she said, and pressed her fingers to his lips when it appeared as though he would say more. "Don't make promises you can't keep." She traced the line of his firm, irresistible lips with her fingertips. "Just touch me." Her tone softened to a whispered demand. "Want me."

"With all my heart."

His admission was a fervent caress against her mouth. His lips shaped to hers in a kiss that shattered Beth's fears into so many inconsequential pieces. She wove her fingers through his hair and held on.

Tyler wanted to tell her he wouldn't hurt her, that losing control now and then didn't have to be a bad thing, that it could be downright erotic between two people in love. But that wasn't what she wanted to hear. The lady obviously didn't want to talk right now.

Neither did he.

His hands shaped the curve of her hips, her sides, her back, anchored her to him as he delved the hot, moist promise of her mouth. She tasted of burgundy wine, sultry and intoxicating. Her fingers in his hair clenched, sending tiny stabs of pain through his scalp that heightened his senses and made him demand more. Her fevered moan caressed his pallet as she moved against him. The sweet flame of her impatience licked from her body to his, becoming his to endure.

But endurance was fickle, patience elusive. Tyler's hands shook as he searched for a clasp or zipper among the sequins of her dress. He growled his frustration when he found none.

Beth's lips curved beneath his. "It's elastic."

She would have said more, would have teased him perhaps over his dilemma, like a teenager fumbling with his first bra hook, but the brush of his fingers when he hooked them over the sequined band at her breasts had her concentrating on drawing in air instead. She clutched the corded muscles of his shoulders as he slid the dress down to her waist, held her breath as his hands roamed up her ribcage, and exhaled sharply when his warm palms cupped her.

She'd forgotten what it felt like. A man's hands. Broad fingers, urgent and intimate. She closed her eyes and stifled the predatory little groan of pleasure that rose in her as he held her, caressed her, his mouth exploring.

It isn't supposed to be like this, she thought, her fingers kneading, her body aching. Not this frantic. Not this out of control.

As if he'd read her mind, Tyler lifted his head. His lips grazed her cheek, found her ear. "Did you think it would be any other way?" he whispered.

Beth stilled.

Tyler drew back. "What is it?"

Beth shook her head, helpless to explain the brief shift in reality at hearing him speak the words he'd said to her so many times in her sleep. "It's a dream I've been having."

"Am I in it?" He stroked the side of her neck, sending yet another delicious shiver through her.

"You come for me," she said, her voice softly husky. "You save me from the fire."

He pushed his fingers into her hair, his crooked smile almost grim. "The only fire around here, lady, is the one you've ignited in me." He massaged her nape, his action soothing yet at the same time arousing. His gray eyes skimmed downward and Beth felt her nipples tighten.

Tyler couldn't resist dipping his head and tasting their honey.

Beth's fingers curled almost painfully into his shoulders. "That's not fair," she said on a ragged breath.

Tyler smiled silently, kissed her collarbone, her throat, her jaw. "What's not fair, sweet one?" His hand at her nape tipped her head back so he could kiss her mouth again.

Beth made a desperate sound deep in her throat. "I can't touch you," she protested against his lips. He felt her tug futilely at the buttons of his shirt. "I want to touch you—" she nipped his lower lip, then ran her tongue over it, "—the way you touch me."

"I'd like that, Beth. I want you to do whatever pleases you." His mouth moved over hers, enticing. "I'll do anything you ask."

His words sent a thrill through her and brought a smile to her lips. She pulled his dress shirt and T-shirt free of his trousers, deliberately allowing her knuckles to graze the fine hairs that arrowed down his abdomen, reveled when his skin trembled at her touch.

"Anything?" she asked.

His eyes glinted like points of silver. "Nothing's off limits."

A wave of heat rushed through Beth. She'd meant to tease, but the man wasn't playing. The look he gave her promised sinful, scandalous things, the sorts of things fantasies were made of but couldn't possibly happen, not in a rational world.

"Tyler—"

"It's all right." He brushed his fingers along her cheek. "Trust me."

I do. God save me, I do.

Determined, desperate to get his clothes off him, Beth pushed his shirt down over his shoulders, realizing too late she'd forgotten to loosen his cuffs.

A trace of a smile tugged at the corners of his mouth. "Let me help you." He removed his shirt and tossed it aside, then pulled his T-shirt up over his head.

Beth stopped breathing. He'd called her beautiful, but he was the beautiful one. She pressed her palms to his broad chest, trailed her fingers over his stomach, taut as an athlete's, then back up to tangle in the fine dark hair between his pectoral muscles. Giving in to temptation, she dipped her head and grazed a rimmed nipple with her teeth.

Tyler sucked in a ragged breath and gripped the back of the bench seat. He'd seen her aroused, tasted her passion, but this unguarded aggression, her willingness to touch him, stirred him beyond anything he could have imagined.

"Beth—"

"Hmm?" She didn't look at him, choosing instead to flick her tongue over his other nipple.

Tyler grabbed her by the shoulders, and at her startled expression, kissed her long and hard. "Do you know what you're doing to me?" he asked, his voice raw with the need to possess her, to own her, body and soul.

Panic flashed in her wide green eyes.

Tyler cupped her face in his hands. "I want to wrap myself in you," he murmured, kissed her eyelids when they fluttered closed. "I want to see your face as I fill you." He pressed his mouth to the corner of hers. "I want to hear you cry out."

She whispered softly against his lips, one word only, but it was enough to launch Tyler's pulse.

"Yes."

She helped him work her dress down over her hips, then slipped out of her black heels and nylons, until skimpy black panties were all that remained. Her skin was smooth and fair against the burgundy velvet seat, and Tyler thought he had never seen such perfection. The lilac rose he'd chosen for this night paled in comparison. He glided his hands up the curve of her calves, over her knees, and higher. Her abdomen tightened as he slowly pulled the wisp of lace free of her hips, but there was no self-consciousness in her eyes when they met his. They were as steady and evocative as a cat's.

Her hair had come loose and framed her heart-shaped face in wild flames. "Fire," Tyler said, tunneling a hand in it. "Like the flames you stir in my heart."

Beth knew the intensity of those flames, had felt them in her dreams, could feel them now through his fingertips. They fanned an urgency in her, a desire so hot she thought perhaps she would die if she didn't have this man, feel his body joined with hers.

She reached for his belt, then exhaled another soft protest when she discovered her fingers were too unsteady to work the buckle. Tyler did it for her. Again, Beth had to force air into her lungs at the sight of him, the power of his perfectly male body. She wrapped her arms around his neck and he eased her back onto the seat.

He poised above her, hands pressing into the cushions beside her shoulders. "Do you know how much I want you?" he asked.

Again, Beth's lips curved in a small smile. "I have a pretty good idea." She slipped her hand downward and curled her fingers around the silken length of him. A sense of power shot through her at the way his eyes darkened, became like smoke, then closed with his tortured groan.

"I've been wanting to do this," she whispered, stroking him. "I've wanted to touch you this way."

She told him he was beautiful as she found the condom she'd tucked in her evening bag. She told him what she wanted from him, and what she wanted to do for him as she unrolled the protective sheath over him.

Tyler lowered his forehead to hers. "Lady, you're driving me crazy."

"Then let's go together." Beth wrapped her legs around his hips and arched into him. "Fill me," she said, shamelessly.

Tyler's control exploded like ashes in a sudden gale. His mouth found hers. His hands buried in her hair, as he buried himself in her. She was liquid and hot. He felt her cry out against his mouth, might have stopped even though it would have killed him, but she arched beneath him, demanding more. A shudder wracked his body and he plunged deeper, and deeper still, until she had taken all of him into her tight heat.

Nothing had prepared Beth for the fire that raged from his body to hers. He did more than fill her, he possessed her. He tore his mouth from hers to whisper things to her, intimate, wonderful, secret things. She tried to tell him what he was doing to her, but there were no words to express the primeval, basic, animal feelings he stirred. She cried his name, but it sounded like someone else's voice. She was a stranger to herself, his rhythmic, driving force taking her to a place she'd never been before.

So this is what insanity feels like.

They were falling, but she wasn't alarmed. Her dreams had prepared her for the feeling of gravity and space in this man's arms. She clung to him as he tucked an arm around her waist, the other around her shoulders, and rolled off the seat. For an instant she was on top of him, his body absorbing the shock of their landing. Then they rolled again, and she was looking up at his glistening torso, his black hair casting a wild shadow over his face. He cupped her bottom in his broad hands and lifted her hips, surged inside her, until Beth felt as though her very soul had been breached.

"Trust me," she heard him whisper for the second time. "Love me."

Always.

Then everything shattered around her.

Tyler felt her climax rip through her into him an instant before his own explosive release. He emptied himself, gave her his heart and soul with one final, shuddering thrust.

Breathless and stunned, he eased down beside her on the carpet and drew her close. She curled into him, resting her head on his shoulder. Tyler stroked her back and considered the overwhelming chemistry between them, the bond that had been forged.

He wondered if she was aware of it.

She shifted and grumbled softly.

"Are you all right?" he murmured.

"I think I have a rug burn."

He kissed her hair. "You can have the top next time."

"Okay."

The second fire was a slow blaze that burned deep and long as they explored and discovered and demanded. He let her have the top, and any other position she wanted to try. And sometime in the night, Tyler found his lost heart.

It had been there all along, tattooed to his lady's lovely bottom.

12

Beth opened her eyes to a patch of stars surrounded by velvet a few feet above her. Disoriented, she tried to sit up, but a weight across her stomach and thighs had her pinned. Realization came in a warm rush. Swiveling her head, she found Tyler's face inches from hers, his eyes closed, his features relaxed in slumber. He lay on his side, his body spooned to hers beneath the blanket he'd covered them with, his arm and leg flung over her possessively.

He looks so innocent, Beth thought, studying his features in the semi-darkness.

But there'd been nothing innocent about his love-making. He'd been late meeting her at Juliet's because he'd stopped to buy condoms.

Another wave of warmth flooded through Beth as the evening they'd shared replayed itself in her mind. Tyler had spread a lap robe on the floor, then made her laugh when he'd darted from the car naked to get another blanket from the trunk. He'd come back inside shivering and coaxed her to warm him. A simple gesture that had rapidly developed into much more. He'd said things to her, wicked, sensual, tender things, touched her in ways she'd never imagined possible. Sometime during the course of the evening, he'd served her champagne in a paper cup, and fed her chocolates. No, there'd been nothing innocent in his actions. He'd known exactly what he was doing.

She'd been afraid of losing herself to him. Looking at him now, his handsome face shadowed with dark whiskers, his mussed hair like black silk in the starlight, his body warm and male against hers, she wanted him still. *I am lost.* Her longing for him had gotten out of control. He'd given everything, and demanded the same in return.

Too much.

Despair and panic gripped Beth. Again, she attempted to sit up, driven by a sudden sense of urgency.

Tyler's arm tightened around her, drew her closer to him.

"Shh," he soothed, his warm breath stirring the hair over her ear. He nuzzled it out of his way and pressed his lips to the sensitive shell.

She stilled, helpless against the desires he so easily aroused in her.

"Tell me about your dream," he whispered.

"There's nothing to tell."

"Do we make love in it?" He sucked her earlobe, sending a sensuous flutter through her.

"Yes," she breathed.

"Before or after I save you from the fire?"

Beth sighed. "After."

"So you give yourself to me out of gratitude." Tyler smiled against her ear.

She punched his shoulder. "Dream on."

It was a playful punch, her soft drawl teasing, and Tyler knew that, for the moment at least, he'd made her forget about running. He'd felt the panic shoot through her and it scared the hell out of him. He couldn't lose this woman. Not now.

"Tell me more about the fire," he quietly urged. "Is it in a building?"

"Outside. It's dark. There are stars overhead." Her voice became pensive and so low it was barely above a whisper. "The fire surrounds me. There's only one way out, but I can't go that way."

Tyler felt the tension seep back into her body. He gently stroked her arm. "Why not?"

"Because he's there."

She shuddered against him and Tyler instinctively knew who haunted her dream. "Your ex-husband."

She drew back and looked at him, as though surprised he'd guessed so easily. *My sweet lady, if you only knew how transparent you've become to me.*

"I can go to him," she said, settling back into the hollow of his shoulder, "or burn." She stared up at the moonroof, her features taut. "I choose to burn."

Tyler lifted a hand to her cheek, caressed it, tenderly grazed his thumb across her mouth, her chin, then back to her mouth. Her eyelashes fluttered shut, the tension in her face relaxing. "Is that where I come in?" he asked.

Another resigned sigh passed between her lips. "You ride up on a huge white horse and carry me away."

A white horse, a white limousine. The symbolism would have been pretty hard to miss. Tyler smiled to himself. "Like in a fairy tale."

"Call it what you want," she said impatiently, as though he'd gotten a little too close to something private. "A fairy tale. A dream. Either way, it's not real. It doesn't mean anything."

Tyler would have argued with her. That she unconsciously perceived him as her hero meant a hell of a lot to him, even if she didn't want to admit to it. But he wondered why she felt the need to be rescued from a man she claimed was part of her past.

Unless there was something about that past she'd left unresolved. In spite of her bitterness over the way her ex-husband had treated her, did she still harbor feelings for the man?

Tyler tucked her closer. She smelled of wild roses and sex. He closed his mind to the sensations that threatened to distract him. Not an easy task. She was warm and pliant, her body fitting to his in a way that would tempt even a saint. And after the evening they'd shared, she was his and his alone.

Still, he asked, "What made you decide to finally end your marriage?"

"Pot roast."

"Pardon?"

Beth took advantage of his momentary

confusion to pull out of his embrace and sit up. She couldn't think straight when he was touching her. Her feelings were too raw. She drew a corner of the blanket with her, pulling it up to cover her breasts and hugging herself to keep it in place.

Tyler leaned against the back seat to face her. Beth's troubled thoughts were temporarily diverted by his nakedness—the muscled arms that had held her tenderly, the bruise on his neck where she'd bitten him, again, the sheen of his broad chest, his taut waist and the arrow of black hair from his navel downward. The blanket draped his lap casually, barely concealing. His body stirred beneath it, as if responding to her attention. Beth quickly brought her eyes up. He was watching her, waiting, his gray eyes like quicksilver in the muted light. Beth looked away and impatiently pushed a hand through her tangled hair, still clutching the blanket with the other.

"Eric wanted pot roast for dinner," she explained, the bitter memory knotting her stomach and bringing a sharpness to her voice. "He knew how I hated it. He knew how many times I'd tried and failed to fix it the way he liked it. Medium rare." It sounded so stupid now, she thought, containing the harsh derision that rose in her throat. Stupid and childish and tragic.

"If I suggested something else, he'd get a long face and ask me why I couldn't do one simple thing for him without making an issue of it." Oh, how she'd detested that face and the way he'd accuse her of not caring, when all along it had been him who hadn't cared.

"So you gave in."

She jerked, anger flaring in her eyes. "You don't know what it was like!"

Tyler took the brunt of her fury with outward calm. But inside, he seethed with a rage of his own. He knew that if ever given the opportunity, he would kill for what she'd suffered, and not lose any sleep over it.

"I know you," he told her evenly. "I know how it must have galled you to go against your nature that way, to submit for the sake of a little peace."

She stared at him for a long moment, clearly surprised this time, and perhaps a little troubled, that he understood her so well.

"Yes," she finally admitted, her voice a tight whisper. She drew in a long, ragged breath and stared out the side window. "I went to the meat market and bought a four pound roast. I followed the instructions in the cookbook, just like I had a dozen times before. When I took it out of the oven and sliced into it, all I could do was stand there and cry." Her brows pulled low, her mouth becoming a tight line. "I'd failed again."

"You didn't fail, Beth."

"Yes, I did!" The pain and anguish in her eyes when she turned and looked at him had Tyler wanting to wrap her in his arms and protect her from her demons. But she would resent him for it, even fight him. She needed to vent her anger, not be coddled.

"I followed the directions!" She was nearly shouting now. "Why couldn't I do it? Why did it have to be such a stupid issue?" she demanded. "Unless I—" Her voice broke and she stopped. A tear rolled down first one cheek then the other and she gave each a furious swipe with the back of her hand. "Unless," she said with stony resolve, "I didn't love my husband enough."

"That's him talking, not you," Tyler said roughly. He moved to sit beside her. Her body was rigid and cold when he pulled her into his arms. She resisted, but he refused to let her go. He wasn't about to let her suffer alone. Not anymore.

"I know you, Elizabeth. I know your

conviction, your strength of will. I won't believe for a minute you didn't do everything in your power to save your marriage."

She stilled. Tyler felt her tear roll down his chest.

"I hate failure," she muttered.

He stroked her hair and back. "I know, baby. I know." Slowly, she began to relax against him. Tyler continued to soothe her, massaging her nape, planting small kisses on her temple. He held her tighter, hating his next question, but needing the answer.

"What did Eric do when he found out?"

"I don't know," she said simply. "By the time he got home, I'd already left."

Beth pulled out of Tyler's embrace and gave another futile attempt to push her fingers through her hair. It was hopelessly tangled. *I must look awful*, she thought, suddenly desperately weary. She let her hand drop.

"After I'd cried for awhile," she went on, determined to finish, "something inside me snapped. I took the butcher's knife and began stabbing the roast. I stabbed and stabbed—"

Again she was forced to stop, the sudden lump in her throat making it impossible to speak. She glanced down at her right hand clenched tightly in her lap. The knuckles were white. That the feelings were still so strong stunned her. She could still see the mangled, over-cooked remains of the roast on the cutting board, and the deep gashes she'd made in the board itself. She could see the knife in her hands, her fingers like a vise on its contoured handle, her reflection in the steel harsh and ugly. She relived the gut-wrenching horror that had drained the blood from her, leaving her cold and shaking.

She willed her fingers to open, and looked at Tyler. The love in his beautiful face tore at her heart. *He doesn't know me. He doesn't know the rage that devoured me.*

But he deserved to. It was the only way to make him understand.

"If Eric had walked through the door while I had that knife in my hands, I would have stabbed him, too," she said with a certainty that was frightening in its coldness. "That's when I realized how much of a stranger I'd become to myself. How out of control the whole pathetic situation had gotten. It scared me," she admitted, her voice haunted. "I scared me. I didn't know who I was, or what I was capable of anymore."

It all fell into place, her fierce need to do things her way, her compulsion toward independence, her resistance to loving him. But most of all, her overwhelming need to remain in control. Tyler had been to that place, had experienced the same helpless rage. He remembered the night he'd planned to kill his father after being beaten for forgetting to take the trash out. He'd gone to the basement and found the old man's eight-pound sledge hammer, intending to bash the bastard's head in. But he'd been too weak from the beating to carry the hammer up the stairs.

He gently brushed a strand of hair from Beth's face and noticed his hand was shaking. "And that's when you left?" he asked.

She leaned into his touch for a moment, then turned away to stare out the window again. "I dumped the roast in the garbage, washed the knife and put it away, packed what I could get into the car and didn't stop until I was...here."

Judging by the size of her car, she hadn't taken much. Some clothes, perhaps, and one old Santa. Tyler's heart cried for her. It hadn't been fair. Nothing about what she'd gone through had been fair or deserved.

"Did he try to come after you?"

"I lived in terror that he would. I called my mother to let her know I was all right." Beth closed her eyes, remembering their conversation and the emptiness she'd felt afterward. "She tried to talk me into coming back. She didn't understand why Eric and I couldn't work things out."

"Didn't she know what kind of man he was? What he was doing to you?"

Beth turned and met the compassion in Tyler's eyes, something her mother had lacked. At least at first.

"She thought I was over-reacting when I tried to explain it to her. It wasn't until a month after I'd left and Eric started *dating*, that she began to see him for what he really was." Beth's short laugh was bitter. "I'd spent five years of my life trying to please my husband, thinking he loved me in spite of our problems. But after I left, he didn't make any effort to find me. It was as though I'd never existed." Unwanted hurt and anger blurred her vision and she looked away. "It was all so...demoralizing."

Tyler's fingers close around hers, his touch warm and strong, yet heart-breakingly gentle. "You can't blame yourself, Beth."

"I was a fool."

"Eric was the fool," Tyler argued, making no attempt to hide his opinion of the man in his voice. He reached out and tilted Beth's chin until she was looking him in the eyes. "Only a fool would try to change you," he told her. He leaned forward and kissed her forehead, her cheek, the corners of her mouth. "Only a fool would tamper with perfection." Her lips parted and he kissed her with all the tenderness of a lover desperate to prove himself.

"I'm not perfect, Tyler," she whispered.

"Neither am I." His hand drifted downward, to her warm, full breast. He brushed his palm across the responding peak. "But I intend to keep trying," he promised.

The look in her green eyes shifted, became predatory. She gripped the hair at the back of his head and pulled his mouth down hard on hers. There was nothing gentle in the way she kissed him, her lips demanding. Almost angry. As though she meant to make him pay for the feelings he stirred in her. Tyler accepted it. Her rage, her pain, her desperation, poured from her into him. She took his mouth with a savage intensity that burned through him. He struggled to keep his response gentle, but desire hooked its claws into him and he felt himself becoming its prey. Beth's prey. She was his desire. Her need was his, her hunger his to satiate. They were headed toward another explosion, and if he was surprised at all, it was at realizing he still had more to give.

He knew the exact moment her anger became heated passion. He could taste it on her lips. Her frustration as she struggled with it, her sighed curse against his mouth as she gave in to it. He shamelessly took advantage, caressing, tasting, demanding more. He wanted her to know just how much he loved her and how much he needed her to love him. He wanted her to know as he held her, as he filled her, that his heart would never be the same because of her.

~~~

Tyler promised her breakfast. Eggs over easy, bacon, and her favorite, buttermilk pancakes. Because it was four o'clock in the morning, Beth had expected some small restaurant that never closed. Instead, he'd taken her to his house and donned a bright red chef's apron over his T-shirt and rumpled trousers.

He'd given her his white shirt to wear over her dress. It hung half-way to her knees. His scent lingered on the soft fabric as she sat at the small kitchen table with her chin propped in her hand, her nose burrowed in the shirt's cuffs, and watched him pour batter onto a griddle. She was intimately aware of his tall, athletic body, the play of muscle in his bare arms, the unconscious grace of his long legs. He was barefoot and his hair mussed, as if he'd just gotten out of bed.

Which wasn't far from the truth. Except they'd gotten very little sleep. Heat rushed through Beth. She'd practically attacked him the last time. He'd made her furious with his need to know, his understanding and gentleness, his kisses that clouded her mind and had her senses crying for more. And he'd given it, willingly, until she'd been certain there was nothing more to give.

She'd been wrong.

The sizzle of the griddle when Tyler flipped another pancake drew her from her reverie. Her stomach rumbled. She really did like having a man cook for her, she decided. The simple, cream-colored kitchen, with its tall cupboards and turquoise accents, was cozy and warm. She gave a sigh of contentment and let the silken cocoon of euphoria wrap itself around her.

"What are you thinking about?"

She blinked and realized Tyler had caught her smiling to herself. "I was just wondering how you manage to do that," she said in a sleep-softened voice.

"What? Flip pancakes?"

"Look so sexy this early in the morning." Her matter-of-factness surprised her. But then she'd done a lot of surprising things lately.

Tyler's eyes went the color of smoke behind his heavy-lidded gaze. "I think lack of sleep has affected your eyesight." His dimpled smile took a seductive slant. "But you won't find me trying to change your mind."

Like a figure from a sweet dream, he crossed the room and pulled her to her feet. She went into his arms as if it were the most natural thing to do. He kissed her, thoroughly, intimately. *He's so good at that.* Beth ignored the little voice that warned her not to get used to it. At the moment, she didn't care about tomorrow or complications. She wound her arms around his neck and kissed him back, her lips lingering, savoring the now-familiar taste of him, the rasp of his unshaven face against her skin. He cupped her bottom and drew her into him, letting her know his desire for her was still very much awake and ready to please.

"I can't get enough of you," he murmured. "You're an obsession."

"You sound like a perfume commercial." Her lips curved against his.

His low chuckle rumbled up his chest. "I'm

trying to turn the lady on and she makes jokes."

"Oh, I'm already turned on."

Tyler gave a low growl and claimed her mouth. Beth felt thoroughly savored, her bones turning to liquid honey, as his heat consumed her. She found herself wondering what it would be like to make love on a kitchen floor.

"What's burning?"

I am, Beth thought for the fraction of a second it took her to realize the question had come from across the room. She tore her mouth from Tyler's to stare at Holly standing in the doorway in red-striped pajamas. The daughter of the man she'd just spent the night with. An incredible, passionate night. The daughter of the man she'd been ready to seduce where they stood. If Holly had walked in on them just a few seconds later...

Heat rocketed up Beth's neck and into her face. She glanced at Tyler and saw the color beneath the surface of his dark whiskers as well. He pulled back slightly, so their bodies were no longer making contact, but his hands at her hips continued to hold her in front of him, and Beth realized his arousal was still a little too obvious for him to pull away completely. The craving was there in his eyes when they met hers. Familiar and private. Not of how it might be, but of how it had been between them.

And would be again, those eyes promised, before they slid from her to his daughter. "What are you doing up so early?"

Holly shrugged. "I smelled food."

Tyler's gaze jerked to the smoking griddle. "Damn," he muttered, and shot across the room to rescue breakfast.

Attempting to regain a shred of composure, Beth pulled the front of her shirt closed and sat, and almost missed the chair.

Holly yawned and smiled at her. "Good morning."

Beth scooted the other half of her rear onto the seat, barely refraining from laughing at the sight she must make. "Good morning, Holly."

If the young woman noticed Beth's flustered state, she had the good manners not to say anything. She shuffled to the stove where her dad was scraping at the blackened pancakes. "Did you just get home?" she asked, a look of innocent curiosity in her expression.

"We got in a little while ago," Tyler answered, giving the griddle more attention than Beth figured it was worth.

Holly tucked her long hair behind her ear

and made a face at the plate of pancakes. "You aren't planning to eat those, are you?"

"No." Tyler turned and dumped the lot in the garbage at the end of the counter.

This time Beth did laugh, making Tyler and Holly look at her. "They remind me of some Christmas cookies I tried to bake," she explained.

Tyler smiled. "Except that Bo isn't here to beg for the burnt remains."

"Where is that big sweetie?" Holly asked.

"My friend Sammy is watching him."

"Oh." Holly looked from Beth to her dad. "Well...I guess I'll just, you know, go up to my room." She took a backward step toward the door.

"Have breakfast with us." The invitation came from Beth.

"I wouldn't want to be in the way or anything. I mean you two looked like you were—"

"Sit down, Holly." Tyler shot his daughter a warning look.

Again she shrugged. "Okay."

Beth's feeling of euphoria returned as she shared an early-morning meal with Tyler and his daughter around the small kitchen table. They made an odd trio, Holly in her PJs, Tyler in the rumpled remains of his uniform, and she in her sequined dress, high heels and man's white shirt. And yet Beth couldn't remember the last time she'd felt this content, as if she truly belonged here.

If Holly had any thoughts about her dad being out all night, she kept them to herself, devoting most of her energy to eating. Beth was pleasantly surprised at the young woman's appetite. She'd thought most teenage girls starved themselves to be thin. It was nice to see Tyler's daughter used more sense. And it kept Beth from feeling guilty as she reached for another pancake, when she'd had three already.

The subject of college didn't come up and Beth decided to leave it at that, for the time being. For all she knew, Holly had spoken to her dad and the matter was already settled.

"Are we still going to get a tree today?" the girl asked, stuffing another strip of bacon into her mouth.

"That was the plan," Tyler said. "How about it, Beth? Would you like to join us in our search for the perfect tree?" He added a dramatic touch to the last part, drawing a disparaging look from his daughter.

Beth smiled at the exchange. "I really should

go home and check on Bo." She gave a self-conscious glance at her attire. "And I'd need to shower and change."

"No problem. I'll drop you off at your place after breakfast and give you some time to do what you need to do. Holly and I will pick you and Bo up later, say around nine?"

"Please say yes, Beth. It would be fun."

Holly's eagerness was infectious. And meeting Tyler's gaze, Beth knew she wasn't ready to let go of the fantasy yet.

"I'd love to," she said.

~~~

Sam's pickup wasn't in the driveway when Tyler parked the Jeep behind Beth's car. Bo Diddley barked at them from the back yard. It was a little before six a.m. and still dark out.

"That's odd," Beth said. "Where would she be this time of the morning?"

The concern in her voice had Tyler scanning the front of the house. The door was closed. No broken glass, that he could see. He opened his door. "I'm coming in with you."

They went around to the back first, to check on Bo. The shepherd met them at the gate, his tail whipping excitedly.

"Hey there, Mr. Diddley," Beth greeted. "Where's Auntie Sam?"

Bo woofed once, as if to answer her. Unfortunately, Tyler mused, he didn't speak shepherd. But the dog wasn't acting like anything was wrong. And the back of the house appeared intact.

They went inside and found Sam's note on the refrigerator.

Dear Bethie,

   Had to drive out to Mom's. She's having one of her crying spells. Bo's had breakfast and I took him for a walk before I left. Want to hear all about you and Ty when I get home!

   See ya later,

   Sam

"So," Tyler said, relieved the mystery had been solved and that, except perhaps for Sam's mom, everything was all right, "what are you going to tell your friend about me?" He'd stood behind Beth, reading the note over her shoulder. It was the perfect position from which to brush her hair back and press his lips to the side of her neck, just below her ear.

She closed her eyes and let her head fall back on his shoulder. "Nothing," she said on a sigh.

"Nothing?" Tyler tried to sound offended as he pushed her coat out of the way and kissed the junction of her collarbone. She sagged against him, as though her knees had gone weak. Tyler wrapped his arm around her waist and drew her closer.

"Mmm," she said on a soft moan, "Sam can get her own fantasy."

"How long do these 'spells' usually last?" Tyler asked, his lips grazing Beth's bared shoulder.

"All day." Her voice had become breathless and husky. "Sammy's mother is a chronic worrier."

Tyler was relentless in his exploration of her satin-smooth skin, trailing kisses from her shoulder to her neck and down to the crimson wing tip of the phoenix on her back.

"It's safe to assume we won't be interrupted then?" he asked. He spread his hand low on her abdomen and pressed her bottom into the saddle of his legs, making her aware of the hard, persistent ache he had for her there.

She sucked in a sharp breath and murmured his name on the exhale. She rubbed against him even as she reminded, "Your daughter's expecting you right back."

His hands slid inside her coat, skimmed up her ribcage, over her breasts, to the top band of her dress. "Then we'll have to shower fast, won't we?"

13

Beth blushed furiously when she answered the door to Holly and her father promptly at nine. The look in Tyler's eyes was positively sinful. The trail of clothes they'd left from the kitchen to the bathroom, the frantic explosion of their love-making in the shower, the sensual way he'd lathered every inch of her body afterward, and she him, blazed in those magnetic depths.

"Good morning, pretty lady. You ready to go?"

Joy bubbled in Beth's slightly breathless laugh. "I'll get my coat."

They went to a tree farm outside of Troutdale, a small community east of Portland. The day had dawned clear and cold, the foursome's breaths puffing in the crisp morning air. They trudged through acres of Nobles and Douglas firs. Dew-moistened branches left wet tracks on their pant legs and droplets on Bo Diddley's muzzle and back. The clean fragrance of evergreens and fresh pitch filled their nostrils. Tyler led the way, wielding a small bowsaw, examining and dismissing tree after tree. Beth and Holly followed along behind and did their best to keep Bo from watering the surrounding shrubbery.

"We go through this every year," Holly said. "Dad really gets into this Christmas thing. Guess it's because he never had much of one when he was a kid."

The comment tugged at Beth's heart. "It's also the day his daughter was born," she offered.

"Yeah," Holly's love for her father reflected in the soft curve of her mouth, "that too."

Tyler finally found his perfect tree, a fat Douglas fir that was miles too tall to fit through the door when they got it home.

"Surprise, surprise," Holly drawled, then squealed when her dad threatened to tackle her on the front lawn.

"Why don't you show Beth where the ornaments are," he told her, "while Bo and I make a few minor modifications to the tree."

"Minor?" Holly rolled her eyes, making Beth laugh. "Sure, Dad."

Beth followed Holly inside and upstairs. She caught a quick glimpse of a room with dark masculine furnishings on the right, a small lavender bathroom, then a brighter room done in pastels to her left, as they made their way down the short, carpeted hall to a room at the end.

"This is partly Dad's office," Holly explained, gesturing toward a neatly organized desk and computer that took up most of one wall, "and partly storage." She threw open the doors of a wide closet stuffed with boxes and miscellaneous items—a pair of skis, a couple of sleeping bags, a tattered suitcase, and what looked like an old 8mm projector.

Bits of Tyler's life, Beth thought, her gaze drawn to a small box marked "photographs." She would have loved a few minutes alone to peek inside, perhaps discover pictures of Tyler as a child, a teenager, a young man. She'd never felt compelled to know the few men she'd been involved with since her divorce, had never wanted to get that close. Doing so would have revealed too much of herself. But with Tyler, it was different. She wanted to know more about this man she was so attracted to. She'd told him things about herself she'd told no other. She'd let him into her heart.

She'd fallen in love with him.

"It's this one," Holly said, breaking into her thoughts.

Beth suppressed the edge of panic that had her in its grip. She helped Tyler's daughter extract a large box from the middle of a stack near the front.

I can't be in love. It's too soon. Too sudden.

She and Holly carried the huge box of ornaments downstairs. Tyler had gotten the tree into the family room and was holding it upright in the corner. Beth took one look at him standing there, tall and sexy in worn blue jeans and a heavy flannel shirt, his arresting gray eyes and his boyish, dimpled grin aimed directly at her, and knew she was lying to herself. She did love him.

The question now was, what was she going to do about it?

She and Holly set the box on the coffee table. Bo Diddley trotted over to sniff it from corner to corner. Beth stepped back, wrapping her arms around her middle, suddenly feeling at odds.

"Beth?"

She blinked and met the concern in Tyler's expression from across the room.

"Is anything wrong?" he asked.

He's such a beautiful, complicated man, she thought. And she loved him with her whole heart. Never had she felt such joy and despair.

"I'm just a little tired." The truth, as far as it went. She was exhausted. Perhaps that was the reason for her confused emotions.

He sent her a private look, as if to tell her he understood. But how could he, when she didn't understand herself?

"We'll take a break and have some lunch soon," he promised. "Somewhere in that box are some lights. Would you see if you can find them while Holly and I get the tree set in its stand?"

"Of course."

Keep busy. That's the trick. Don't allow the doubts time to set root.

With renewed determination, Beth lifted the lid off the box and felt a jolt from the past take her breath. Delicate glass ornaments with pearl glaze and hand-painted scenes framed in gold and silver glitter lay in protective pockets of tissue. She lifted one and examined it in the light that streamed through the front window.

It was so fine she could almost see through it. So much like the ones her grandmother had given her. Blown glass Santas and teardrops with miniature scenes inside.

All gone now. Victims of her sham of a marriage. She closed her eyes and held the fragile bobble to the sudden tightness in her chest. How long would it be before Tyler started rearranging her life? Or would she be the first to mess things up?

She felt him move behind her, breathed in his woodsy, male scent. It would be so easy to lean into him, say to hell with the doubts that crowded her mind. But for how long?

"More ghosts?" he murmured.

She opened her eyes to find him watching her reflection in the window. He knows. And as much as he tried to hide it, she could see his frustration.

She turned and took a step back, returning the ornament to its box to avoid looking at him. "I think Bo and I should go home now."

"But the tree hasn't been decorated."

Beth heard the disappointment and underlying anger in Tyler's carefully controlled voice. It couldn't be helped. She needed time. She needed sleep. Heaven help her, she needed him.

"I don't want to intrude on this time with your daughter anymore than I already have," she said over the swell of hopelessness in her throat.

He stepped in and tucked a finger under her chin, lifting her gaze to his. His touch was gentle, electric. "You're not intruding, Beth."

The emotion laid bare in his eyes was devastating. "Tyler, I—"

"You can't go," Holly interrupted. She was standing next to the tree with a forlorn expression on her face. "I mean, not yet." She looked from Beth to her dad and back. "I have something I wanted to talk to Dad about and I kinda wanted you to be here."

Tyler lowered his hand and turned to face his daughter. "What is it, Holly?"

Beth thought she knew. She felt the room close in on her. *Not now*, she silently pleaded. *I can't deal with this now*. "Holly, I really don't think—"

"I've made a decision about college," the girl stated, ignoring Beth's feeble protest. She squared her shoulders and met her father's look. "I'm not going."

Tyler pushed his hands through his hair and gave a sigh of exasperation. "Holly, we've been over this a dozen times. Why are you bringing it up now?"

Holly's eyes flicked to Beth, then back to her dad. Beth thought she saw the girl's chin lift slightly in an effort to bolster her courage. "You've been after me to make a decision," she answered. "Well, I've made it."

"I wanted you to decide which college to go to." The patience in Tyler's voice was strained. "Not going at all wasn't an option."

"Well, it should be."

"Well, it's not! We'll talk about this later."

Beth saw Holly's chin tremble and wondered if Tyler was aware of it.

"I don't want to go to college," the girl pressed, "and you could use that money to expand the business."

Tyler shook his head. "Absolutely not."

"Why?" The tremble had crept into her voice.

"Because I said so."

Tears welled in Holly's eyes. Fists clenched at her sides, she cried, "I don't know why I try talking to you! You won't listen to anything I say!" Her gaze flew to Beth, accusing and hurt. "Didn't I tell you?"

She sobbed and ran upstairs. A door slammed. The silence that followed was deafening. Beth chewed at her lower lip and felt the pull of Tyler's stare. Slowly, she looked at him. Fatigue had settled in the lines of his face. Anger and confusion battled in his gray eyes gone to steel.

"Would you mind telling me what that was all about?" he asked with deceiving calm.

Beth sensed the thin thread that held his temper in check. She decided tact was the best approach. "Holly and I talked a little about college. She mentioned she didn't want to go."

"Did she happen to mention that her grandmother willed her savings to be used for tuition?"

Beth didn't like his condescending tone. When she answered, her own voice was deliberate and even. "No. She did not."

"I didn't think so." Tyler massaged the bridge of his nose as if briefly giving in to weariness, then dropped his hand and met her gaze. "Holly's been given an opportunity I never had. I won't let her throw that away."

"It sounds to me like you're expecting her to make up for your mistakes."

"Not make up for," he corrected, "learn from. I want what's best for my daughter. She has the chance for a better life and I mean to see she gets it."

"By making her decisions for her?"

"This one, yes," he said adamantly. He moved to the bookcase, stared at the framed photographs there a moment before picking up the one of a little dark-haired girl in a frilly summer dress. "I was Holly's age when I made the decision to drop out of school and become a father. I did it because I wasn't getting the love and guidance I needed at home. I won't make that mistake with my own child." He returned the photograph to its place on top of the bookcase and turned. "There's a difference between parental guidance and manipulation, Beth."

Her back stiffened. "I never said—"

"You didn't have to. You think I'm trying to control my daughter, the way your husband controlled you."

"My marriage has nothing to do with this."

"Doesn't it?" He moved closer. "You're still blaming yourself for putting your trust in the wrong man, and you're determined to see that Holly doesn't make the same mistake."

"That's not true," Beth insisted. The idea was absurd. But she didn't like the edge of desperation she heard in her voice. She'd only been trying to help.

Hadn't she?

Her feeling of claustrophobia returned with

a vengeance. She backed away, wrapping her arms around herself again, and began to pace like a caged animal. "I offered some advice," she said.

Tyler stepped in front of her so she was forced to stop and look up at him. "From the first day we met, you've blamed me for things someone else did to you. Well, I've got a news flash for you, Beth. I'm not your ex-husband. If you're angry with him, take it out on him, not me. And leave my daughter out of it."

A feeling of finality, as unyielding and cold as granite, closed around Beth's heart. She drew in a deep breath and tried to control the desperation, the feeling of impotence, that settled in every cell of her body. It was all falling apart around her, just as she'd known it would.

But it shouldn't have ended like this. Not this quickly. And not in anger. But like sand through her fingers, she couldn't seem to stop it from happening.

She looked away and started for the door, grabbing her jacket and Bo Diddley's leash as she went. "Come, Bo," she commanded solemnly. The dog fell into step beside her.

"How do you plan on getting home?"

"I'll walk," she stated without breaking

stride.

She heard his muttered curse seconds before she slammed the door behind her. The noonday sun sent sharp pains stabbing through her dry, weary eyes. She made her way blindly down the drive to the sidewalk. Memories pursued her, memories of inadequacy, of being smothered, of slowly dying inside. Her feet moved faster, as though she could outrun the feelings that haunted her. Bo broke into a trot to keep up.

They'd almost made it to the end of the block when Tyler drove the Jeep up over the curb and across the sidewalk in front of them. He leaned over and opened the passenger door.

"Get in."

She did. Not just because the look in his eyes brooked no argument, but because refusing would have been self-defeating and foolish. It was less than five miles from his house to hers, but in her exhausted state, she doubted she could have made even one.

And Bo had already planted himself in the back seat.

It was a silent fifteen-minute drive. Tension crackled like the dry heat before a lightning storm. Tyler's features were set in stone, his attention fixed on the road. Beth held her back rigid, her jaw clenched so tightly her temples began to throb.

The man wasn't being reasonable. Did he expect her to simply forget the lessons she'd learned from her marriage? Sweep them under the rug as if they'd never happened?

She couldn't do that. Not for any man.

Her nerves were strung as taut as piano wire by the time Tyler pulled up in front of her house. Beth had her door open before the Jeep had even come to a complete stop. But when she tried to climb out, Tyler grabbed her upper arm and held her fast against the seat.

Bo stood in the back and growled.

"Call him off," Tyler said, his voice low and even.

Beth looked down at the broad, strong fingers wrapped around the sleeve of her jacket, then up. His anger was very much alive in his eyes. But there was more. A naked vulnerability that left her stunned.

"It's all right, boy," she murmured. "Sit."

The shepherd did as he was told, but his steady gaze never left the man.

"What do you want from me?" Beth asked, her tone bitter. "An apology?"

"I want to hear you say my name."

She shook her head, confused.

"Who am I?" he demanded in that same low voice. But it had lost some of its evenness.

"Tyler Stone," Beth said quietly.

Some emotion she couldn't identify flicked across his expression, then was gone. "Just so you know who it is you're running from," he said and abruptly released her arm.

Myself. She even opened her mouth to tell him so. But the feelings were too close to the surface, too raw.

And he was too angry.

She got out of the Jeep and ordered Bo to follow. Slowly, she made her way up the walk to the porch and let herself and the shepherd in. It wasn't until she'd closed the door behind her that she heard Tyler drive away.

Out of her life.

14

Beth tucked a cable-knit sweat in the open suitcase on the couch and tried once more to convince herself she wasn't running. She'd rearranged her schedule for this vacation weeks ago, long before Tyler had ever entered her life and turned it upside-down.

Long before his accusations.

She swallowed the despair in her throat and went to her bedroom for another pair of socks. Bo Diddley followed at her heels as if afraid she'd leave without him should he let her out of his sight. He always enjoyed their yearly retreat, Beth mused. It had become a tradition with them. Ten days of peace and solitude in the mountains. Just the two of them.

The way it will always be if you leave now.

Returning to the front room, she uttered a growl of frustration and threw the rolled socks at the suitcase in an overhand pitch that would have impressed a pro. Bo sat with an uneasy whimper. Releasing a weary-heavy sigh, Beth knelt and hugged him.

"It's all right, boy. I'm not mad at you."

He acknowledged her apology by putting a paw on her shoulder and licking her chin.

And then because she simply couldn't remain on her feet another minute, she sat next to him on the carpet, and leaned her back against the couch. She hadn't slept or eaten since Tyler had dropped her off that afternoon, almost twelve hours ago. How could she, when her stable, ordered life had been thrown into turmoil?

It's your own fault.

Bo dropped to his belly and laid his head in her lap, rolling his big eyes up at her. Beth absently scratched him between the ears and came to the unavoidable conclusion that it was herself she was angry with. Oh, she disapproved of the way Tyler had completely ignored his daughter's feelings. And his accusations that her failed marriage had somehow influenced her advice to the girl were totally unfair.

But what really troubled her was that she cared. She'd ignored the common sense she'd come to rely on, and had allowed herself to fall in love with an impossibly head-strong man and his equally head-strong, confused daughter.

And now you're running.

The truth was persistent. Beth massaged her temple. Her brain felt on the brink of an overload. If only she could sleep.

The doorbell rang and she jumped. Bo stood and gave a low growl, his full attention focused on the front door. Beth glanced at the clock above the television as she got to her feet. It was after one in the morning. Sammy would still be at the club.

Hooking her fingers through Bo's collar, she made her way toward the door, her steps slow and cautious, her pulse drumming in her ears.

"Who is it?" she demanded.

"It's me."

The sound of Tyler's voice made her heart stop, then race. She felt the tension leave Bo's body, and his tail began to wag. Indecision paralyzed her. What was he doing here at this hour? Did she want to see him? What would she say to him?

"Beth?"

An edge of worry had crept into his voice. Beth opened the door.

Her breath caught at his haggard appearance. Deep lines etched the tight slash of his mouth and the corners of his burnished eyes. His hair was spiked as though he'd run his fingers through it often. And he needed another shave, his rigid jaw shadowed by dark stubble. He seemed oblivious to the frosty night air in a sweat-dampened T-shirt, faded blue jeans and a pair of tattered white high-tops.

As if he'd been doing some running of his own, Beth thought. A lump formed in her throat at how glad she was to see him. "You look awful," she said.

"I've been playing basketball." His voice had a husky rasp to it. "Can we talk?"

Beth nodded and stepped aside.

Tyler hadn't been sure she'd open the door to him, much less invite him in. Even now, he didn't know how she felt about him. And after the things he'd said to her earlier, he wouldn't have been at all surprised if she'd decided to call the police on him. He felt Bo's wet nose nudge the back of his hand as he stepped inside, but it was the open suitcase on the couch that caught and held his attention.

Something hard and cold formed in the pit of his stomach.

I'm too late.

"You're really going, then," he said dully.

"I'm on vacation." She turned and moved to the couch.

Tyler stood at the edge of the room and watched her rearrange the contents of the suitcase. She wore the same snug jeans and bulky sweatshirt she'd had on earlier, and had pulled her fiery hair into a relaxed ponytail at the back of her head, exposing the delicate curve of her neck. He ached just looking at her.

"You didn't mention a vacation before."

Before we spent the night together. Made love. Argued.

He saw the color high on her cheekbones deepen as she re-rolled a pair of thick pink socks.

"I had...other things on my mind," she said without looking at him.

Tyler wanted to believe he'd been more than just a distraction to her. He stepped closer and murmured, "I'm sorry, Elizabeth."

"You were only being honest about your feelings."

"I was being cruel."

This time she did look at him. For an instant.

Then her gaze slid away. But not before Tyler saw the confusion in her green eyes.

She gave a small shrug. "Sometimes the truth hurts."

"Damn it, Beth—" She flinched and he stopped. Raking his fingers through his hair, he took a deep breath and blurted, "I was jealous."

She looked up, a frown drawing her finely arched brows together. "Jealous? Of what?"

"You." There was no humor in his short laugh. "All this time I was worried about how Holly would react if I brought a woman into our home. It never occurred to me that I might be uncomfortable with my daughter suddenly having someone besides me to confide in."

"It took me by surprise as much as it did you," Beth admitted. She perched on the edge of the couch next to her suitcase, like a nervous bird about to take flight. Bo seemed to sense her distress and moved to her side, laying his head in her lap. Beth ran her hand over the shepherd's back.

"How is Holly?" she asked.

"She's not speaking to me."

"I'm sorry, Tyler. I had no idea she would do something like this."

Tyler crossed the room and knelt in front of

her. He rubbed Bo between the ears, careful not to let his hand touch Beth's. He knew if he did, he'd forget why he was here.

"Will you tell me now what the two of you talked about that day on the mountain?"

"She wanted to know if my parents made me go to college."

"Did they?"

"No."

There was no accusation in her voice. Still, Tyler felt a short stab of guilt. "You said you offered Holly advice."

"I suggested she take some courses at a community college until she found something she was interested in."

"You've been there, Beth." Tyler was unable to hide the note of impatience in his voice. "I thought you, of all people, would know how important it is."

"I had a goal. Holly doesn't."

"A flibbertigibbet." He stood and moved restlessly across the room.

"Pardon?"

"Grandma used to call her a flibbertigibbet because she'd flit from one interest to another. Basketball, volleyball, drama, track, half a dozen different art classes. She was good at everything she tried. But then she'd get bored and drop it."

A brief, sympathetic smile flicked across Beth's expression. "Would it be so bad if she didn't go to college right away?"

Tyler drew in a deep breath, held it a second, then released it in a rush. "I'm afraid if she doesn't go now, she never will."

"That's her choice."

"But her grandmother—"

"Is dead," Beth gently interrupted. "Holly's got her whole life ahead of her. Don't break her spirit by forcing her to do something she doesn't feel in her heart."

"Why could she talk to you and not me?" Tyler asked.

Beth gave a sad smile. "Because you've got your heart set and you're only hearing what you want to hear."

Tyler responded with an arid, defeated laugh. "She doesn't want to go to college."

"And she doesn't want to hurt you. She's not in the habit of disobeying you, Tyler. She loves you too much for that."

He knew what she said was true. He didn't understand why it hadn't occurred to him before now. "You know my daughter better than I do."

Beth shook her head. "I have the advantage

of distance. Sometimes it's easier to see things if you're not too close."

Tyler felt the cold, hard lump in his stomach shift. He realized she was referring to his relationship with his daughter, but she may as well have been talking about the course their own relationship had taken.

He eyed the suitcase, then her. "Is that why you're leaving? Because things were getting 'too close'?" He wasn't quite able to keep the bitterness from his voice. That she could even consider leaving now, after he'd given her his heart, hurt deeper than any beating he'd ever received at his father's hand.

He saw the fleeting look of panic in her eyes.

She stood and began to pace. "I told you, I'm on vacation."

"For how long? Where are you going?"

"I can't tell you."

Tyler bit back the feeling of helplessness that threatened the tight control he had on his temper. "Can't or won't?"

"Does it matter?"

"It matters a hell of a lot to me."

"Please, Tyler," she wrapped her arms around her middle in a defensive gesture he'd come to recognize, "I need time to myself."

"I thought that's what I was giving you

when I stayed away last week."

The shadow of an achingly sad smile pulled at her features. "And you made up for it by not letting me out of your sight for more than an hour since."

"Funny," he said, though his tone lacked any suggestion of humor, "I thought you wanted it that way as much as I did. You seemed to be enjoying yourself."

"I did. I was. But it's all happening too fast, can't you see?" She stopped pacing and looked at him. "I feel suffocated."

He tried not to show how much that hurt. "If I held on too tight—"

"Yes. You did."

"It was only because I was afraid of losing you." Tyler swallowed the hopelessness that swelled in his throat. "I feel you slipping away and I don't know what else to do."

"Let me go," she said softly.

"I don't know if I can do that."

"You don't have a choice, Tyler."

She reached out as though she would touch him and his breath caught. He could almost feel her caress, the softness of her fingertips against his skin. But she withdrew her hand at the last second and it was all he could do to keep from crying out.

"You said some things I need time to think about," she told him. "I'm not doing this to hurt you. Believe me, that's the last thing I want to do."

He did believe her. But it didn't stop the hurt from clamping around his heart like a vise and squeezing. He cursed his big mouth, yet he couldn't take back the words. He'd meant everything he'd said.

"You do what you feel you have to," he finally told her. "But before you go, there's something I want you to have." He dug in the coin pocket of his jeans for the small gold band. "I had planned on giving it to you tomorrow. I thought you would be spending Christmas with us." He saw her wince. He hadn't intended it, but he wasn't sorry. He held the ring out to her. "It belonged to my grandmother."

Beth stared at it. "I can't."

"You could if you married me."

Her head came up, shock carved in every beautiful feature. "I care for you a great deal, Tyler, but I thought you understood. Marriage is out of the question."

If her words had hurt before, this time they slashed deep and jagged through him. "I know why you believe it is," he said. His fingers curled around the ring until the metal bit into his palm. "Remind me to kill that ex-husband of yours if I ever meet up with him."

She shook her head wearily. "Why do you keep insisting Eric has something to do with this?"

"Doesn't he?"

"No!"

"Then let him go."

"I left the state and filed for divorce," she said, her voice heavy with sarcasm. "What more do you want?"

"Get rid of the baggage you brought with you," he said. "You've devoted your life to healing other peoples' scars, but it's time you took a good look at your own." He closed the short distance between them, almost touching, but not quite. "You may think that bird on your back has released you from the past, but it's a myth. It's going to take more than a piece of paper and a pretty tattoo to set your heart free."

"You don't know what you're talking about." But the desperation in her voice gave her away.

"I need you," Tyler said, sounding just as desperate. "Holly needs you." It was dirty pool and he knew it, but he wasn't feeling very noble at the moment. "I love you, Elizabeth."

"Don't say that!"

"I love you and there isn't a damn thing you or I can do about it!" He wasn't sure why he was shouting. Maybe because she was. Or because if he didn't, the frustration and pain would explode through his chest.

Or maybe he just didn't like having his heart ripped out.

Bo shifted on his haunches and gave a worried growl. He's as confused as I am, Tyler thought. Looking at Beth was like looking at a mirror image of himself, the despair and anguish he was feeling at that moment reflected in her expression. He wanted to gather her in his arms and hold her to him until her heart admitted what her head denied.

But doubt held him back.

"I can't make you love me," he said, his voice lowering to a tired, coarse whisper. "I can't make you say the words. But I know what we have is right. I just hope you figure it out before it's too late." Then because there didn't seem to be anything more to say, he turned and left.

As Tyler closed the door behind him, Beth felt a void open in her heart. If he'd kissed her, she would have given in. But he hadn't. He hadn't even touched her. She had the feeling she knew what it had cost him.

It wasn't until she'd moved to secure the deadbolt that she saw the ring on the small table by the door. She picked it up with great care, as if were made of the finest glass. It was a simple band with delicate leaves etched in antique gold.

But it was more than just a ring. It was an heirloom, a symbol of the love two people had shared years ago. She imagined it in Tyler's strong, capable hand as he slipped in on her finger and promised to love, honor and cherish.

She should have known the man wouldn't play fair.

Her vision blurred and she wept.

~~~

The snow was half a foot deep along the banks of the Sandy River. The rocky south bank rose steeply for thirty feet to a row of rustic homes, secluded from each other by thick fir trees, their broad branches bowing under the weight of the snow. Beth looked out the picture window of one of these homes and felt as if she were the last person on earth. The rushing waters of the river directly below her front deck camouflaged the sounds of traffic from the four-lane highway a hundred yards behind the house. A short way to the east, where the opposite bank of the river met the water more gradually, a large log cabin nestled in the trees, but no smoke rose from its chimney. Her own small fireplace in the corner of the room crackled with a cozy blaze that only seemed to intensify her isolation.

She blinked and realized Bo Diddley was watching her from the deck, a mound of snow on the end of his nose and his tongue lolling happily. Beth gave him a half-hearted smile.

"Hey, silly," she called through the glass, "what have you been up to?"

The shepherd's tail rotored like a helicopter blade. He woofed once and trotted off to continue his exploration.

Beth sighed and turned away from the window. It was the day after Christmas, and except for Bo, she was alone. She'd succumbed to exhaustion shortly after arriving two days ago. Fourteen hours of blessed unconsciousness. For the first time in weeks, she hadn't dreamed. Even in sleep, loneliness enveloped her.

She looked around her, at the familiar room with its knotty pine walls, hand-crafted furnishings of twisted willow branches and neutral broadcloth cushions, the river-rock fireplace and hearth, and felt as though she'd come full circle, ending up right where she'd started. There was no Christmas tree, no decorations. She'd brought the gifts she'd been given with her from Portland and had quietly opened them yesterday. Sam did buy her a blazer the evening they'd gone shopping at the mall, but not the salmon pink one that had been on display. Instead, she'd chosen a conservative navy wool with a matching skirt. Her mother had sent her a beautiful rose comforter and coordinating sheets.

And then there was the ring.

She looked down at the circle of gold in her hand. She couldn't remember having picked it up, but it always seemed to be in her grasp. Her heart constricted. She'd known the first time she'd laid eyes on the man, the deceiving innocence of his handsome face beneath the shadow of his garrison cap, he would be trouble. But she'd never expected this.

Of course she couldn't marry him. She didn't believe in love ever after. And she would never again sacrifice her freedom, her identity, for the sake of a man. She'd only brought the ring along because she hadn't wanted to risk misplacing it. That it occasionally found its way onto her finger was inconsequential. After all, it was beautiful.

And a perfect fit.

Oh dear, she thought, her legs crumpling beneath her so she was suddenly sitting on the hardwood floor. *I do want to marry him.* She'd realized it the moment she'd heard him drive away, the sound of the Jeep's engine fading into heart-numbing silence. The thought of living the rest of her life without Tyler in it filled her with a horrible desolation.

Then why couldn't she put Bo in the car and drive back to Portland and tell him?

Because nothing had changed. Because Tyler's accusations were true. She was afraid of love, afraid of its potentially destructive nature. It was easier to take the things Tyler had done out of caring and compassion and twist them into something ugly and manipulative, than to admit she loved him. Her failed marriage had done that to her. Even now, four years after her divorce, Eric still controlled her.

My phoenix is a lie, she thought, remembering Tyler's words.

Something else he'd told her flashed through her mind. *If you're angry with Eric, take it out on him, not me.*

At the time, she'd been too upset to see the logic of his challenge. But now it made perfect sense. She'd been too hurt, too demoralized and insecure the day she'd fled her marriage to tell Eric just what she thought of him. She'd bottled it inside her where it had fermented and grown into something bitter and unpalatable, like wine gone to vinegar. She could continue on the way she had been and become a sour, lonely old woman, or she could release the bonds that held her phoenix heart captive.

I know what we have is right. I just hope you figure it out before it's too late.

A sense of urgency had her standing. She began to pace between the window and hearth. How late was too late? she wondered. Tyler had said he loved her, but how long before his patience wore out and he demanded she return the ring? For all she knew, he wanted it back now, but he had no way of knowing where it, or she, was. Would his love hold out a few more days? Until she could do what needed to be done?

It was a chance she'd have to take. This was something she had to do for herself, for her future, regardless of whether or not her relationship with Tyler could be salvaged.

She reached for the phone and called her mother.

~~~

Wilson Investment Services was located in Seattle's business center. The streets were terraced along a hillside overlooking the harbor. But on the morning Beth arrived, a thick blanket of fog lay heavy over the city. The tangy smell of sea air salted a chilly breeze that promised snow. Beth didn't allow herself time to dwell on how empty she felt returning to her home town, or how insane her plan was. Her mother had tried to talk her out of it, which was why she'd stayed at the condo only long enough to drop off her over-night bag, promising they'd discuss the matter when she returned.

Beth's pulse drummed in her ears as she pushed through the wide glass doors and entered the lobby of the brokerage firm that was the financial foundation of the Wilson family. The feeling of having stepped into a reoccurring nightmare struck hard and she had to stop just inside to give her equilibrium a moment to recover. For some reason, she'd expected the place to have changed. The dark green carpet, the bright-white walls with framed posters of the Space Needle, Mt.

Rainier and Olympic National Park, the imitation leather chairs and glass-topped end tables littered with magazines. It was as if the past four years had never happened. She was almost afraid to check the dates on the tattered *National Geographic* and *Sports Illustrated*.

"May I help you?"

Beth's attention swung to the desk at her right. A pretty, young blond in a smart black suit eyed her expectantly. She, at least, was new, Beth thought with a small measure of relief. Not that it surprised her. Long term alliances were simply beyond the Wilson family's grasp, even in business.

Beth finger-combed her wind-tossed hair and straightened the front of her wool blazer and skirt. "I'm here to see Eric Wilson. Is he in?"

"Yes. Do you have an appointment?"

"No. Is he alone?"

"I believe so, but—"

"Thank you." Beth started toward the back offices with measured, determined steps.

"Wait a minute! You can't go in there without an appointment!"

Beth ignored the woman. She passed the first two doors without slowing. Those offices belonged to John and Harris Wilson, Eric's father and older brother, respectively. Eric's was at the end of the hall. The nameplate on the closed door confirmed it. Beth hesitated, drew in a deep, steadying breath, the weight of her future suddenly pressing in on her. Wiping her clammy palms down the sides of her skirt, she turned the doorknob just as the receptionist caught up with her.

"I'm sorry, Mr. Wilson," the young woman said, pushing into the room ahead of Beth. "I tried to stop her."

Eric sat behind a dark mahogany desk, a phone to his ear, his attention on the computer monitor in front of him. It was easy for Beth to see what had first attracted her to him. He had classic features that age had only enhanced — straight, aquiline nose, full sensual mouth, sculptured jaw. He still wore his sun-streaked blond hair cut conservatively short and combed back from his high forehead, which at the moment, was marred by a deep scowl.

Over being interrupted, no doubt, Beth thought.

He looked up. His piercing blue eyes stared at her, then widened as recognition set in. It was as if an icy breeze swept through the room and over her. Beth resisted the urge to wrap her arms around herself and returned his stare.

"It's all right, Marsha," he said, not breaking eye contact. "Close the door on your way out." Then remembering the phone in his hand, he said brusquely, "I'll call you back," and hung up.

He stood slowly and came around the desk. His dark gray suit fit his height and build perfectly. Of course Beth had expected nothing less. He'd always demanded perfection in himself as strongly as from those around him.

"Well, if this isn't a surprise," he drawled.

"Hello, Eric."

"Lizzy."

Beth's jaw tightened before she could stop it. She'd always disliked his nickname for her. Which was probably why he'd insisted on using it. She'd lost count of the little things he'd done simply because they annoyed her. She watched him cross the room toward her, with his expensive clothes and precisely groomed looks, and felt...nothing. It took her by surprise. She read every nuance in his expression, the way he carried himself, the tone of his voice, and realized how incredibly transparent he was. As though a blindfold had been lifted, she saw him for what he really was for the first time.

"What are you doing here?"

"I was in the neighborhood—"

"That's crap."

Beth's smile was cool. "You're right, it is." She allowed her gaze to slide down his trim frame, then up—a slow perusal, as if accessing a piece of merchandise—empowered by her newly discovered immunity to him.

"You're looking good," she remarked, "but then you always did."

He made a derisive sound deep in his throat. "Thanks. What have you done to your hair?"

His question was precisely what she'd expected and she answered with a sharp-edged laugh. "I cut it. You haven't changed a bit, have you?"

"So you've said. I'll ask you again, what are you doing here?"

"It's simple really. I came to take care of some unfinished business."

His pale blond eyebrows dipped. "Isn't it a little late for that?"

Beth ignored his sarcasm. "Better late than never." She began to move slowly around the room, pausing to run her fingers over the tip of a feathery air fern and admire a reproduction of Andrew Wyeth's *Christina's World*, put there to impress his clients. Her ex-husband had never cared a whit about art. Considering her chosen profession, she wondered how on earth they'd ever met.

"Tell me something," she said, turning to look at him. "Have you learned how to like yourself without cutting other people down yet?"

His stance became defensive, arms crossed, legs spread. Beth resisted the urge to laugh at his attempt to intimidate her. She knew the sound would be a bitter one.

"What kind of question is that?"

"I thought it was pretty clear."

"Who the hell do you think you are, coming in here and criticizing me?" he demanded. "You're the one who ran off like a spoiled brat."

"Scared," she quickly corrected.

His frown deepened. "Would you repeat that?"

Beth recognized his tone. It was intended to make her feel stupid. She forced back the ire that rose in her throat. "Scared," she said, louder this time, as if speaking to someone who was hard of hearing, all traces of pleasantness gone from her voice, "not spoiled. Scared of what I was becoming."

"You're not making any sense."

"I don't expect you to understand."

"What's to understand? You barge in here after all this time, talking some nonsense about liking myself and being scared. I haven't got time for this." He spun on the heels of his dark gray oxfords and strode to his desk. "I'm very busy."

"You always were."

This made him stop. He turned and studied her for a long time, his eyes assessing and cold. "Are you implying that it's my fault our marriage didn't work?"

"I wouldn't dream of it. You see, I know how hard it is for you to accept blame."

His gaze narrowed. "Especially where it's not due."

Beth regarded him with the same clinical aloofness he'd afforded her. "Like I said, you haven't changed. You're the same egotistical son of a bitch you were when I met you."

Eric stared at her, as if stunned. Then, characteristic of his controlling nature, he changed tactics. She saw it in his expression, his body language, the subtle shift from aggressor to charmer. He did it to confuse her. It made Beth sick to her stomach to think of all the times it had worked in the past.

But not this time.

His voice was as smooth as cream, his smile

relaxed. "There was a time when you thought differently."

For a moment, Beth thought she would lose her meager breakfast of coffee and toast on his expensive wall-to-wall carpet. She lifted her chin and drew her shoulders back. "I'm willing to admit I made an error in judgment. Can you do the same?"

Eric's mouth twisted. "My only mistake was in thinking you could ever make a good wife."

"Is that why you never bothered to look for me?"

"I did."

"Now who's lying?"

A muscle in his jaw ticked. "I didn't look for you because I knew it would be a waste of time."

"You're right. It would have. But weren't you even the tiniest bit curious why I left?" she asked, baiting him.

"I thought it was pretty obvious," he remarked dryly. "You didn't love me enough."

Something inside Beth snapped. "I did love you!" She took an aggressive step toward him.

He blinked and stepped back before realizing what he was doing and stopped.

Beth didn't care. She advanced another step. "You took that love and made a joke out of it!

Your idea of a good wife was sexist and degrading!"

This time there was no mistaking the astonishment in his expression. "I gave you everything!" He jabbed at the air with a forefinger. "Everything!" he repeated, his voice cracking as it gained volume. "And it was never enough!"

Beth held his gaze and silently counted to five before speaking. "I feel sorry for you," she said, her voice almost a whisper now. "You must be incredibly lonely."

He drew back as if she'd slapped him. "Don't insult me with your misdirected pity."

"Excuse me, I forgot. Pity implies that one is less than perfect and therefore to be pitied. A condition you could never be blamed of."

Eric's face went scarlet. He took a step toward her, his hand raised. For a fleeting second, fear lurched through Beth. He'd never struck her before. But the fear lasted for only a second. Keeping her feet firmly planted, she braced her stance. If there was one thing Sammy had taught her, it was to never let your enemy see your fear. The other was to aim for the groin and eyes.

"Try it," she said with deadly calm.

He stopped. She could see the precarious

balance between rage and uncertainty in his eyes. And something else, she realized. Fear. Eric Wilson was afraid of her! She struggled to control the smile that pulled at her mouth, then gave in to it. Seeing him this way was just too good to resist. It was a dangerous thing to do, but she laughed.

Eric didn't like being laughed at. Past experience had taught her that. His eyes took on a murderous glint, but he didn't come any closer.

"This conversation is over," he finally stated. "I'll have Marsha show you out."

"Don't bother," Beth told him. "I'm already gone."

Standing beside his desk, he looked like a model from the pages of a fashion catalog, handsome, precise and one dimensional. It occurred to her that in their entire conversation, not once had he asked her how she was or where she'd been.

And it didn't matter.

She allowed him one last cool smile. "Goodbye, Eric." Then she turned and started for the door.

"What did you hope to gain by coming here?"

His question made her stop and look back at

him. His bearing was stiff and proud, but underneath, Beth could see his utter bafflement, and for the briefest moment, she found she really did feel sorry for him. The poor man didn't have a clue. He was destined to spend the rest of his life destroying everything that meant anything to him, until he ultimately destroyed himself.

Too bad she wouldn't be around to see it.

"What did I hope to gain?" she repeated thoughtfully. A small smile curved her lips. "Something you'll never have."

He made an impatient gesture with his hand. "And what is that?"

"Peace of mind."

Beth could see he didn't have the slightest idea what she was talking about. "I'd love to stay and explain it to you," she said, "but I have a wedding to go to."

A pang of doubt jarred through her as she turned and reached for the door. She slid her other hand into the pocket of her wool blazer and wrapped her fingers around the small, cool band. Don't let it be too late, she silently prayed.

Then she walked out, closing the door on Eric forever.

15

Rain pelted the super-stretch limousine as it cruised the four-lane highway like a sleek, onyx bullet in the night. A relentless east wind pounded its fists against the heavy car and threatened to turn the rain to snow. The weather suited Tyler's mood. Cold and foul.

Traffic was light. In less than three hours, people would be bringing in the New Year, drinking champagne toasts at parties or celebrating in the privacy of their own homes. For Tyler, it was just another night without Beth in it.

He'd gone through the motions of living, carrying on as though the act of normalcy would make it so. But nothing felt normal with the woman he loved gone. His fingers tightened on the steering wheel of the new black Town Car he'd added to Luxury Coach's fleet three days ago, a purchase he'd made without using Holly's tuition. His daughter didn't know everything about his business. She'd been aware of his desire to expand the fleet, but he hadn't told her of the money he'd been putting aside for it. Telling her wouldn't have made any difference. She would have found some other need, no doubt just as worthy, to spend the money intended for college on. Beth had been right. As much as he wanted the best for his daughter, she was old enough to make her own decisions. And her own mistakes. Trying to force her to do something she didn't want to do had only alienated her, and torn him up inside. So they'd compromised.

He could see now he'd pushed too hard with Beth, also, and driven her away. He should have waited to ask her to marry him. But if patience was a virtue, then he was not a virtuous man. He'd understood her reluctance to commit and had pressed the issue anyway. What hurt was not knowing if she would ever be ready.

I care for you a great deal. She hadn't even been able to say she loved him.

Maybe she didn't.

He pounded the steering wheel with the heal of his hand. "Where the hell are you?" he growled, his voice sounding hollow in the big empty car. Didn't she know how much he worried about her?

She did know. That was the problem. She didn't like being worried over, or protected, or rescued. *Suffocated*. He muttered another soft curse. He couldn't stop the need he had to shelter the ones he loved. It was his nature.

He started when the semi-truck he'd pulled up beside drove through standing water and sprayed the limousine's windshield.

"Miserable weather," he grumbled and pressed his foot to the accelerator, leaving the big rig behind. New Year's Eve or not, why would anybody want to go out on a night like this?

It wasn't just the weather that had him wishing he'd turned this job down. The four-lane stretch of road reminded him of the morning he and Beth and Holly had driven to Government Camp, the fun they'd had and how like a family they'd been. He wanted those things back.

The woman who had called to set up this evening's appointment had insisted Tyler

Stone be her chauffeur. Something about a friend of a friend giving him a good reference. He hadn't been interested enough to pursue the details. It didn't matter. None of it mattered. He was just going through the motions.

It was then he noticed the precipitation reflected in the limo's headlamps had taken on a fat, white appearance.

"Great," he muttered humorlessly. "Nothing like a little snow to keep the evening interesting."

Seconds later, he drove through the Welches Road intersection and began looking for the turnoff he'd been told to take. There, on the left, beneath a single streetlight. Tyler tapped the brakes, signaled and turned onto a dark, narrow road that curved back and paralleled the highway. He could make out houses in the trees on both sides. All but a couple of them appeared unoccupied. Vacation homes. He realized too late he hadn't confirmed the condition of the road and whether or not there would be a place big enough to maneuver the long car around. But even as he thought it, the road ended in a wide culdesac.

The address he'd been given was the last house on the right. Lights at the front and side illuminated a wide deck that wrapped around the small, single-level cabin. Tyler backed into the gravel drive and parked in front of a compact garage.

Buttoning the front of his black, sheepskin-lined car coat, he pulled the bill of his garrison cap low on his forehead, and got out. An icy wind bit at his face and hands. He could hear the strong current of the Sandy River over the rustling trees, but couldn't tell how close it was. He glanced in the direction of the sound, but the darkness was impenetrable beyond the lights of the house.

A powdering of white lay over the two inch crust that remained of an earlier snowfall and made walking chancy in his slick-soled oxfords. He skirted what must have once been a snowman, reduced now to a melted lump beside the deck, and climbed the steps. When he reached the door, it opened.

His heart surged into his throat. "Beth?"

She looked like heaven, her lovely features glowing in the dancing firelight from across the room. Her red-gold hair shimmered about her face and brushed the slope of her ivory shoulders, bared by the low cut of a simple, long-sleeved black knit dress that hugged her full breasts and trim waist, then flared at the curve of her hips, stopping mid-calf. Incongruous to her slender dress, and sexy as hell, thick white socks bunched at her ankles.

Tyler stared, convinced he was dreaming, afraid if he blinked, she'd vanish.

"I should have warned you," she said softly. There was uncertainty in her low, mellow voice and the way her green eyes searched his. "I had Marie make the appointment. I wanted to surprise you." She stopped to nervously moisten her lips. "Tyler, I'm sor—"

"It's really you," he whispered, cutting through her apology.

A tentative smile played at the corners of her mouth. "Yes."

Tyler sucked in a breath so sharp it hurt. "God, I've missed you."

Beth had convinced herself he wouldn't want to see her, other than to ask for his ring back, that this crazy scheme had been a mistake. She'd paced the floor upon her return from Seattle that afternoon, rationalizing, doubting, agonizing. She'd even picked up the phone twice to call Marie and tell her to cancel tonight's appointment. But the husky break in Tyler's voice, the smoky look in his eyes that told her he was as hungry for her as she for him, had her glad she'd hung up both times before completing the call.

"I've missed you, too," she said.

He started through the door even as she reached for the front of his coat and pulled him inside. He kicked the door shut with the heel of his shoe and hauled her against him. He was solid and real beneath his heavy coat and Beth thrilled at the feel of him, the rediscovery of his touch, his embrace.

"I've missed you so much," she repeated fervently, tears brimming her eyes.

"I was worried."

"I know."

Beth wondered how she could have ever mistaken his tenderness, his love, for anything less. A tear spilled down her cheek. Tyler dipped his head and pressed his lips to it. They were cool, hesitant.

"I can't help how I feel," he told her.

"Shh." Beth pushed her fingers through the hair on either side of his head, causing his garrison cap to tumble to the floor, and drew his mouth toward hers. "We'll talk about it later."

Desire flared in his smoke-gray eyes. "All right."

His words were a warm caress that laid claim to the inner recesses of her parted lips.

There was nothing hesitant in the action this time, his kiss quickly heating to an intensity that incinerated any lingering reservations Beth might have had about inviting him here, about opening her last defense to him.

"Bo's not going to run in and attack me, is he?" There was fierce possession in the way Tyler's mouth moved over hers, explosive and overwhelming.

Like he was kissing her for the first time.

It was the first time, Beth decided, because she wasn't the same woman.

"Bo's in town with Sam," she told him breathlessly, reluctant to break the domination of his lips for even a second.

His groan of approval shivered through her.

Urgency vibrated in the air, the desperate need to satisfy a fundamental hunger that had been denied too long. With very little persuasion, Tyler's coat and suit jacket joined his cap on the floor. Beth tugged at the buttons of his shirt, pulling him farther into the room at the same time. She heard one pop, then another, before she had the shirt off of him.

It took a little longer to get him out of his trousers, and she really should have helped him with his shoes first. Stumbling and laughing, he managed to shed the last of his clothes, while Beth skimmed her hands over his taut shoulders and back.

Then it was her turn. The dress she wore buttoned down the front. But not for long. Her single article of lingerie, a pair of black lace panties, quickly followed the puddle of her dress to the floor. Her thick socks stayed on.

Tyler's skin was hot, his lean body hard when he gathered her to him again. His lips trailed a sensual path from her mouth to her throat. Beth grabbed his shoulders for support, her knees melting beneath her.

"Where's the bedroom?" he breathed between sucking her earlobe and running his fingers down the small of her back.

"Who cares?" she asked on a soft moan.

Tyler's answer was a low growl against her neck. Holding her, kissing her, he guided her to the thick rug in front of the couch.

It was a heated union, driven by impatience and separation, fanned by the winds of passion and love. I love this man, Beth thought, her heart nearly breaking at realizing just how much. The future was still an unknown. She could still lose him. Only this moment was certain, his body filling her as she drew him deeper with each thrust. His murmured endearments no longer frightened her with their sweet promises. She would take what he gave, without fear of losing herself. He'd reached into the shadows of her heart and soul, laid her bare. And in return, he had set her free.

She said his name, then said it again because she loved the sound of it.

"Trust me," he murmured against her mouth.

"I do," she whispered back. "I do."

And then they went beyond the ability to speak, their bodies communicating what couldn't be put into words.

Tyler felt her completion shudder through her on the crest of his own. He held her until her body stilled, then eased down beside her on the rug and tucked her to him. She laid her head on his shoulder and spread her fingers across his damp chest, her hand small and tender.

And trusting. She trusted him. A calm settled over him. He held her, warm and pliant, against him, breathed in her rose scent. He didn't ask the questions that crowded his head for fear of breaking the euphoric spell that had wrapped itself around them. He caressed her softly tangled hair and stared at the dwindling fire.

Incredibly, he realized he'd dozed off when Beth shivered and stirred at his side.

"How long have I been asleep?" he asked.

"Not long." She brushed her lips over his cheek. "But the fire's going out."

"Who cares?" He turned his head and captured her mouth.

"You will pretty soon," she replied with a soft laugh. "It's the only thing heating the house."

"Oh really?" Tyler grinned at the two spots of color that appeared high on her cheeks.

"Forget I said that." Her voice was low and throaty, the downward sweep of her lashes endearingly self-conscious. She sat up and reached for his shirt.

Tyler propped himself on an elbow and took pleasure in watching her fumble with the tangled fabric. She finally got the shirt turned right side out and slipped it on, only to give a dismayed groan at the missing buttons.

"It looks like I owe you a new shirt," she said.

"It can be mended."

She glanced at him, her expression bland. "I don't sew."

"I do." Her look of surprise made him chuckle. "I carry a kit in the limo. It's all part of the service."

"You never cease to amaze me," she murmured, a smile gently curving the corners of her mouth.

"That's my plan." He leaned forward and kissed her with all the tenderness of a man who dared to hope. "Maybe you won't get bored with me that way."

Her green eyes sparkled with her small, astonished laugh. "You're the most un-boring man I've ever met," she told him, then stood before he could haul her back to his side.

Tyler enjoyed the way his shirt tucked under the curve of her bottom when she moved away from him. At the stone fireplace, she pushed the long sleeves up to her elbows, brushed her hair away from her face, then placed a stout chunk of wood from the hopper onto the glowing coals. Watching her, he felt a tranquility that had eluded him all his life. Oh, there had been brief moments watching his daughter grow and discover life's mysteries when a certain serenity would come over him. But this was different. He felt complete. He decided he would do whatever she asked of him to hold onto that feeling. To hold onto her. If she wouldn't marry him, he would content himself to being her lover for as long as she would have him.

"I noticed you've got a new limousine." She'd taken a poker from the brass stand next to the fireplace and was pushing at the coals.

Tyler located his trousers and stood to pull them on. "Yes," he replied, then at her questioning glance, added, "I didn't need Holly's tuition."

Beth nodded. She'd already suspected as much. She didn't like the idea that Holly had tried to play her sympathies with the flimsy excuse. She returned the poker to its stand.

"Were the two of you able to work things out?"

"She's been filling out job applications all week."

Surprised, Beth looked at him.

"I don't like it," he said on a sigh, "but I can live with it."

His admission reaffirmed what Beth had come to discover about him, that his love was genuine and came from his heart. That he'd been willing to change, to bend, for the love of his daughter was proof enough. She felt a bottomless peace settle over her.

"I'm glad," she said.

He moved toward her, barefoot and shirtless, his trousers clinging to his lean hips, and her body flooded with desire and love.

"She feels responsible for what happened between us," he said.

"I never meant—"

"Don't ever apologize for caring, Beth." The gentle touch of his hand on her cheek quieted her. "Holly needs somebody like you in her life."

"Somebody like me?"

"Strong, independent—"

"Stubborn," she interrupted with a brief, regretful smile.

"You're a survivor."

She flinched. "Regardless of who it hurts," she muttered, and backed away from his touch before he could stop her.

Folding her arms across her middle, she moved to the window and stood gazing out at the cold, starless night. The blackness was total beyond the reach of the lights that flooded the snow-covered deck. They could have another five or six inches by morning, she thought. How she'd loved to race outside as a child and try to catch as many snowflakes as she could on her tongue. Her dad had always joined her, while her mother got the hot chocolate ready.

"This house belonged to my parents," she said softly. "After Daddy died, Mom signed it over to me. She couldn't take coming here without him."

"She must have loved him very much."

"Yes. She did." Beth couldn't remember a single angry scene between her parents. What she did remember was wishing for that kind of relationship with a man and feeling as though it was her fault for not finding it with Eric.

"It's ironic that what kept Mom away, drew me," she said. "I always felt safe here, as though Daddy's spirit was somehow watching over me. When I left Eric, this was the first place I thought to come."

And it was where she'd run to this time, Tyler realized, staring at her stiff back. But why? Because she'd needed to feel safe from him? Because she'd known he couldn't find her here? The thought was like a knife to his heart.

But he was here now, he told himself. She'd invited him. He clung to that truth and waited for her to continue.

"I went to Seattle." She rubbed her hands up her arms as though suddenly chilled. "I saw Eric."

Tyler felt an uncontrollable stab of jealousy. "How'd it go?" he asked, unable to prevent that jealousy from hardening his voice.

Beth heard it and turned to look at him. He

stood beside the fireplace, the flames casting a bronzed hue over his naked arms and chest. He exuded a raw sensuousness, like a raven-haired warrior, lean and virile and dangerously handsome, and her heart collided with her ribs.

"You were right," she said. "I should have confronted him a long time ago." It was her turn to close the distance between them, approaching Tyler slowly. "I guess I just didn't have a reason to before."

"And now you do?"

The uncertainty in his expression tugged at her. She came to a stop in front of him and gave him a gentle smile.

"You're my reason, Tyler. You and Holly. When I got here this last time, nothing was the same," she confessed. "I realized I had changed and I didn't want to be alone anymore."

She held out her hand to him and he laced his fingers with hers.

"You don't have to be," he said, his voice a husky whisper.

"I know that now. But first I had to prove to myself I was right to walk out of my marriage, that Eric was everything I'd remembered, and that you and he had nothing in common."

"What are you trying to say, Beth?"

"I love you."

Joy ricocheted through Tyler. He lifted their twined hands and brushed his lips across her fingers. "I never thought I'd hear you say it."

"I never thought I would," she admitted, feeling suddenly breathless. "I thought I could survive without love complicating my life." She smiled at her foolishness. "But I hadn't counted on you."

Awareness flared in Tyler's eyes, turning them from steel to smoke. "I haven't changed my mind," he told her. "I want to spend the rest of my life with you. I'll take whatever you're willing to give."

Beth pulled back to reach into a crystal dish on the mantle.

"In that case, you'd better take this." She held the small, gold band out to him. It was his grandmother's ring, he realized, and his heart stopped. Plummeted.

"You'll need it when the justice of the peace tells you to put it on my finger."

Tyler's heart restarted with a jolt. "Are you sure, Elizabeth?"

"I want to marry you, Tyler." She spoke softly, but with conviction. "If you'll still have me."

He gave a triumphant laugh and lifted her

off her feet. Beth threw her arms around his neck, her lips finding their way instinctively to his. She knew the taste of love and happiness as his mouth opened to hers. He belonged to her, every bit as much as she to him. She understood the fierce possessiveness that had driven him to want it all, because it was what she want, too.

"I'll do everything in my power not to suffocate you," he vowed, his low voice fervent as he set her down. He rested his forehead against hers. "But you've got to allow me to do things for you now and then. It's the way I'm made."

"No apologies," she whispered. "I love the way you're made." She kissed him, tenderly. "I thought of a tattoo for you."

"As long as you don't want to put it on my butt."

"No," Beth said, laughing. "I was thinking your shoulder. A knight in armor, right about here." She pressed her lips to a spot on his left deltoid.

"Why a knight?"

"Because that's what you are to me. You charged into my life, so bold and sure of yourself, and rescued me from a lonely existence."

"I wasn't sure of anything," he framed her face to kiss the small crease between her brows, "except that I loved you."

"Why, Tyler?" She drew back, studying him. "When I did everything I could to discourage you, why didn't you give up on me?"

"Your compassion," he said simply. "It's in your work, the way you give yourself to people who need you. I wanted to be a part of that. And I wanted to be the one you came to when you needed somebody to hold you." He pressed his mouth to her forehead. "I wanted to be the first face you saw in the morning and the last one you kissed when you closed your eyes at the end of the day."

His words filled Beth with unspeakable pleasure. "I like the way that sounds," she said, smiling. She pulled out of his arms briefly to retrieve a small, flat package wrapped in red foil and a silver bow. "I haven't given you your Christmas present." She handed the gift to him and watched nervously as he held it, ran his fingertips over the smooth surface. "I wasn't sure what to get you. I know you like to read..."

Tyler thought her uncertainty sweet. Didn't she know he would cherish anything she gave him?

"You didn't have to do this," he said, even as

he began tearing at the pretty paper. It was a copy of *Traveling Through the Dark*, by William Stafford, an Oregon poet. "I don't know what to say, Beth."

"You're right. It was a dumb idea."

She moved to take the book from him, but Tyler held it over his head, out of her reach.

"I happen to like poetry," he informed her.

"You're just saying that to be polite."

"'We shall not cease from exploration,'" he said, quoting a T. S. Elliot line that had stuck with him, "'and the end of all our exploring will be to arrive where we started, and know the place for the first time.'"

Beth stared at him, struck by his words and how close they came to describing her life to this point. She'd spent the last four years exploring, searching for her true self, only to end up where she'd started. And yet everything had changed. It was as though she was seeing it all for the first time. She was the phoenix at last, she realized. And Tyler had been her fire.

"It's a very thoughtful gift," Tyler said, softly breaking into her thoughts. "I'm touched by it." He set the book aside. "I'm touched by you."

She moved into his arms, complete in her happiness and love for him. "Tell me you love me," she said. There was amusement in the smile she gave him. "Without shouting it this time."

"I love you, Elizabeth." The look in his eyes darkened as he whispered it, then dipped his head and moved his mouth over hers. "I love you."

His last declaration was smothered against her lips. But Beth heard it. Her entire being, body and soul, heard it in the way he held her and kissed her.

Then in the distance, she heard other sounds. Car horns and firecrackers. And from across the river, a single trombone. She drew back and smiled.

"Happy New Year, Tyler."

His sexy, dimpled smile had her balance doing crazy things. Love and desire brimmed in his soft gray eyes.

"Yes," he said, his velvet-edged voice like a caress, "it is."

His warm, intimate mouth promised many happy years to come as it shaped to hers. Beth returned his kiss, accepted his promise, trusted in it, in him, and felt her phoenix heart take flight.

The End

About The Author

Cindy Hiday divides her time between mentoring the latest group of writing talent at Mt. Hood Community College and working on the next novel. Currently a member of Willamette Writers, she lives in Oregon with her husband and four-legged friends.

Made in the USA
San Bernardino, CA
21 January 2015